THE PENULTIMATE PERIL

❧ A Series of Unfortunate Events ❧

BOOK the Twelfth

THE PENULTIMATE
PERIL

by LEMONY SNICKET

Illustrations by Brett Helquist

HARPERCOLLINS*Publishers*

www.lemonysnicket.com

ISBN-10: 0-06-441015-3 (trade bdg.)
ISBN-13: 978-0-06-441015-1 (trade bdg.)
ISBN-10: 0-06-029643-7 (lib. bdg.)
ISBN-13: 978-0-06-029643-8 (lib. bdg.)

12 13   CG/RRDH   20 19 18 17

❖

First Edition

For Beatrice—
No one could extinguish my love,
or your house.

CHAPTER One

Certain people have said that the world is like a calm pond, and that anytime a person does even the smallest thing, it is as if a stone has dropped into the pond, spreading circles of ripples further and further out, until the entire world has been changed by one tiny action. If this is true, then the book you are reading now is the perfect thing to drop into a pond. The ripples will spread across the surface of the pond and the world will change for the better, with one less dreadful story for people to read and one more secret hidden at the bottom of a pond, where most people never think of looking. The miserable tale of the Baudelaire orphans will be safe in the pond's murky depths, and you will be happier not to read the grim story I have written, but instead to gaze at the rippling scum that rises to the top of the world.

The Baudelaires themselves, as they rode in the back of a taxi driven by a woman they scarcely knew, might have been happy to jump into a pond themselves, had they known what sort of story lay ahead of them as the automobile made its way among the twisting streets of the city where the orphans had once lived. Violet, Klaus, and Sunny Baudelaire gazed out of the windows of the car, marveling at how little the city had changed since a fire destroyed their home, took the lives of their parents, and created ripples in the Baudelaires' lives that would probably never become calm. As the taxi turned a corner, Violet saw the market where she and her siblings had shopped for ingredients to make dinner for Count Olaf, the notorious villain who had become their guardian after the fire. Even after all this time, with Olaf trying scheme after scheme to get his hands on the enormous fortune the Baudelaire parents had left behind, the market looked the same as the day Justice Strauss, a kindly neighbor and a judge in the High Court, had first taken them there. Towering over the market was an enormous, shiny building that Klaus recognized as 667 Dark Avenue, where the Baudelaires had spent some time under the care of Jerome and Esmé Squalor in an enormous penthouse apartment. It seemed to the middle Baudelaire that the building had not changed one bit since the siblings had first discovered Esmé's treacherous and romantic attachment to Count Olaf. And Sunny Baudelaire, who was still small enough that her view out the window was somewhat restricted, heard the rattle of a manhole cover as the taxi drove over it, and remembered the underground passageway she and her siblings had discovered, which led from the basement of 667 Dark Avenue to the ashen remains of their own home. Like the market and the penthouse, the mystery of this passageway had not changed, even though the Baudelaires had discovered a secret organization known as V.F.D. that the children believed had constructed many such passageways. Each mystery the Baudelaires discovered only revealed another mystery, and another, and another, and several more, and another, as if the three siblings were diving deeper and deeper into a pond, and all the while the city lay calm on the surface, unaware of all the unfortunate events in the orphans' lives. Even now, returning to the city that was once their home, the Baudelaire orphans had solved few of the mysteries overshadowing them. They didn't know where they were headed, for instance, and they scarcely knew anything about the woman driving the automobile except her name.

"You must have thousands of questions, Baudelaires," said Kit Snicket, spinning the steering wheel with her white-gloved hands. Violet, who had adroit technical faculties—a

phrase which here means "a knack for inventing mechanical devices"—admired the automobile's purring machinery as the taxi made a
sharp turn through a large metal gate and pro-
ceeded down a curvy, narrow street lined with
shrubbery. "I wish we had more time to talk, but
it's already Tuesday. As it is you scarcely have
time to eat your important brunch before getting into your concierge disguises and beginning
your observations as flaneurs."

"Concierge?" Violet asked.

"Flaneurs?" Klaus asked.

"Brunch?" Sunny asked.

Kit smiled, and maneuvered the taxi
through another sharp turn. Two books of
poetry skittered off the passenger seat to the
floor of the automobile—*The Walrus and the Car-
penter, and Other Poems* by Lewis Carroll, and *The
Waste Land* by T. S. Eliot. The Baudelaires had
recently received a message in code, and had
used the poetry of Mr. Carroll and Mr. Eliot in
order to decode the message and meet Kit

Snicket on Briny Beach, and now it seemed that perhaps Kit was still talking in riddles. "A great man once said that right, temporarily defeated, is stronger than evil triumphant. Do you understand what that means?"

Violet and Sunny turned to their brother, who was the literary expert in the family. Klaus Baudelaire had read so many books he was practically a walking library, and had recently taken to writing important and interesting facts in a dark blue commonplace book. "I think so," the middle Baudelaire said. "He thinks that good people are more powerful than evil people, even if evil people appear to be winning. Is he a member of V.F.D.?"

"You might say that," Kit said. "Certainly his message applies to our current situation. As you know, our organization split apart some time ago, with much bitterness on both sides."

"The schism," Violet said.

"Yes," Kit agreed with a sigh. "The schism. V.F.D. was once a united group of volunteers,

trying to extinguish fires—both literally and fig-
uratively. But now there are two groups of bitter enemies. Some of us continue to extinguish
fires, but others have turned to much less noble
schemes."

"Olaf," Sunny said. The language skills of
the youngest Baudelaire were still developing,
but everyone in the taxi knew what Sunny
meant when she uttered the name of the notorious villain.

"Count Olaf is one of our enemies," Kit
agreed, peering into her rearview mirror and
frowning, "but there are many, many more who
are equally wicked, or perhaps even more so. If
I'm not mistaken, you met two of them in the
mountains—a man with a beard, but no hair,
and a woman with hair, but no beard. There are
plenty more, with all sorts of hairstyles and
facial ornaments. A long time ago, of course, you
could spot members of V.F.D. by the tattoos on
their ankles. But now there are so many wicked
people it is impossible to keep track of all our

enemies—and all the while they are keeping track of us. In fact, we may have some enemies behind us at this very moment."

The Baudelaires turned to look out of the rear window, and saw another taxi driving behind them at quite a distance. Like Kit Snicket's automobile, the windows of this taxi were tinted, and so the children could not see anything through the darkened glass.

"Why do you think there are enemies in that taxi?" Violet asked.

"A taxi will pick up anyone who signals for one," Kit said. "There are countless wicked people in the world, so it follows that sooner or later a taxi will pick up a wicked person."

"Or a noble one," Klaus pointed out. "Our parents took a taxi to the opera one evening when their car wouldn't start."

"I remember that evening well," Kit replied with a faint smile. "It was a performance of *La Forza del Destino*. Your mother was wearing a red shawl, with long feathers along the edges.

During intermission I followed them to the snack bar and slipped them a box of poison darts before Esmé Squalor could catch me. It was difficult, but as one of my comrades likes to say, 'To be daunted by no difficulty; to keep heart when all have lost it; to go through intrigue spotless; to forgo even ambition when the end is gained—who can say this is not greatness?' And speaking of greatness, please hold on. We can't allow a potential enemy to follow us to our important brunch."

When someone says that their head is spinning, they are usually using an expression which means that they are very confused. Certainly the Baudelaires had occasion to use the expression in this way, after listening to a person hurriedly summarizing the troubles of a splintered secret organization and quoting various historical figures on the subject of wickedness while driving a taxi hurriedly toward some mysterious, unexplained errands. But there are rare moments when the expression "My head is spinning" refers to a time when one's head is actually spinning, and when Kit uttered the word "brunch," one of these moments arrived. The steering wheel clasped firmly in her gloves, Kit turned the taxi so sharply that it spun off the road. The children's heads—along with the rest of their bodies—spun along with the automobile as it veered into the dense, green shrubbery on the side of the road. When the taxi hit the shrubbery it kept spinning, and for a few seconds the siblings saw nothing but a green blur as the car spun through the shrubbery, and heard nothing but the crackle of branches as they scraped along the sides of the car, and felt nothing but relief that they had remembered to wear their seat belts, and then all of a sudden the Baudelaire heads stopped spinning, and they found themselves shaky but safe in a sloping lawn on the other side of the shrubbery, where the taxi had come to a stop. Kit turned off the engine and sighed deeply, leaning her head against the steering wheel.

"I probably shouldn't do that," she said, "in my condition."

"Condition?" Sunny asked.

Kit lifted her head, and turned to fully face the Baudelaires for the first time since they had entered the car. She had a kind face, but there were lines of worry across her brow, and it looked like she hadn't slept properly for quite some time. Her hair was long and messy, and she had two pencils stuck into it at odd angles. She was wearing a very elegant black coat, buttoned up all the way to her chin, but tucked into the lapel was a flower that had seen better days, a phrase which here means "had lost most of its petals and wilted considerably." If the Baudelaires had been asked to guess Kit's condition, they would have said she looked like a woman who had been through much hardship, and the Baudelaires wondered if their own hardships were equally clear in their faces and clothes. "I'm distraught," Kit said, using a word which here means "sad and upset." She opened the door of the taxi and sighed once more. "That's my condition. I'm distraught, and I'm pregnant."

She unhooked her seat belt and stepped out of the car, and the Baudelaires saw she had spoken the truth. Beneath her coat, her belly had a slight but definite curve, as happens when women are expecting children. When a woman is in such a condition, it is best to avoid strain, a word which here means "physical activity that might endanger either the woman or her future offspring." Violet and Klaus could remember when their mother was pregnant with Sunny, and spent her free time lounging on the largest sofa in the Baudelaire library, with their father fetching lemonade and pumpernickel toast, or adjusting the pillows beneath her so she was comfortable. Occasionally, he would play one of their mother's favorite pieces of music on the phonograph, and she would rise from the sofa and dance awkwardly, holding her growing belly and making funny faces at Violet and Klaus as they watched from the doorway, but for the most part the third Baudelaire pregnancy was spent in quiet relaxation. The Baudelaires felt certain their mother had never spun a taxicab through shrubbery during her pregnancy, and were sorry that Kit Snicket's condition did not allow her to avoid the strain of such activities.

"Gather all of your things, Baudelaires," Kit said, "and if you don't mind, I'm going to ask you to carry my things, too—just some books and papers in the front seat. One should never leave any belongings in a taxi, because you can never be sure if you'll see them again. Please be quick about it. Our enemies are likely to turn their taxi around and find us."

Kit turned away from the Baudelaires and began to walk quickly down the sloping lawn, while the Baudelaires looked at one another in bewilderment.

"When we arrived at Briny Beach," Violet said, "and saw the taxi waiting for us, just like the message said, I thought we were finally going to find answers to all of our questions. But

I have more questions now than I ever did."

"Me too," Klaus said. "What does Kit Snicket want with us?"

"What did she mean by concierge disguises?" Violet said.

"What did she mean by observations as flaneurs?" Klaus asked.

"What's so important about brunch?" Violet asked.

"How did she know we met those villains in the mountains?" Klaus asked.

"Where is Quigley Quagmire?" Violet asked, referring to a young man of whom the eldest Baudelaire was particularly fond, who had sent the coded message to the three children.

"Trust?" Sunny said quietly, and this was the most important question of all. By "trust," the youngest Baudelaire meant something along the lines of, "Does Kit Snicket seem like a reliable person, and should we follow her?" and this is often a tricky question to ask about someone. Deciding whether or not to trust a person is like deciding whether or not to climb a tree, because you might get a wonderful view from the highest branch, or you might simply get covered in sap, and for this reason many people choose to spend their time alone and indoors, where it is harder to get a splinter. The Baudelaires did not know very much about Kit Snicket, and so it was difficult to know what their future would be if they followed her down the sloping lawn toward the mysterious errands she had mentioned.

"In the few minutes we've known her," Violet said, "Kit Snicket has driven a taxicab into a mass of shrubbery. Normally I would be unwilling to trust such a person, but . . ."

"The poster," Klaus said, as his sister's voice trailed off. "I remember it, too. Mother said she purchased it during intermission, as a souvenir. She said it was the most interesting time she'd ever had at the opera, and she never wanted to forget it."

"The poster had a picture of a gun," Violet

remembered, "with a trail of smoke forming the words of the title."

Sunny nodded her head. "*La Forza del Destino*," she said.

The three children gazed out at the sloping lawn. Kit Snicket had already walked quite some distance, without looking back to see if the children were following her. Without another word, the siblings reached into the passenger seat and gathered up Kit's things—the two books of poetry they had spotted earlier, and a cardboard folder brimming with papers. Then they turned and began walking across the lawn. From behind the hedges came a faint sound, but the children could not tell if it was a taxicab turning around, or just the wind rustling in the shrubbery.

"*La forza del destino*" is an Italian phrase meaning "the force of destiny," and "destiny" is a word that tends to cause arguments among the people who use it. Some people think destiny is something you cannot escape, such as death, or a cheesecake that has curdled, both of which always turn up sooner or later. Other people think destiny is a time in one's life, such as the moment one becomes an adult, or the instant it becomes necessary to construct a hiding place out of sofa cushions. And still other people think that destiny is an invisible force, like gravity, or a fear of paper cuts, that guides everyone throughout their lives, whether they are embarking on a mysterious errand, doing a treacherous deed, or deciding that a book they have begun reading is too dreadful to finish. In the opera *La Forza del Destino*, various characters argue, fall in love, get married in secret, run away to monasteries, go to war, announce that they will get revenge, engage in duels, and drop a gun on the floor, where it goes off accidentally and kills someone in an incident eerily similar to one that happens in chapter nine of this very book, and all the while they are trying to figure out if any of these troubles are the result of destiny. They wonder and wonder at all the perils in their lives, and when the final curtain is brought down even the audience cannot be sure what all these unfortunate events may mean. The Baudelaire orphans did not know what perils lay ahead of them, as they followed Kit Snicket down the lawn, but they wondered—just as I wondered, on that fateful evening long ago, as I hurried out of the opera house before a certain woman could spot me—if it was the force of destiny that was guiding their story, or something even more mysterious, even more dangerous, and even more unfortunate.

Chapter Two

If you were to hold this book up to a mirror, you would see at once how confusing it is to read letters and words when they are reflected back to you. In fact, the entire world looks confusing in a mirror, almost as if there is a whole other world beyond the shiny silver surface, exactly the same as the world we live in, except backward. Life is perplexing enough without thinking about other worlds staring back at you from the mirror, which is why people who spend a great deal of time looking in the mirror tend to have trouble thinking about anything except whatever secrets they discover after so much reflection, such as a previously unknown sibling who was already watching them at that very moment.

The Baudelaire orphans, of course, had not spent very much time looking in mirrors recently, as they'd been quite preoccupied, a word which here means "in desperate and mysterious circumstances brought about by Count Olaf." But even if they had spent every waking moment staring at their own reflections, they would not have been prepared for the perplexing sight waiting for them at the end of the sloping lawn. When Violet, Klaus, and Sunny at last caught up with Kit Snicket, it felt as if they had stepped into the world on the opposite side of the mirror without even knowing it.

Impossible as it seemed, the lawn deposited the children at the roof of a building, but a building that lay flat on the ground instead of rising up toward the sky. The Baudelaires' shoes were inches from the roof's glittering shingles, where a large sign read HOTEL DENOUEMENT.

Below the sign, farther from the orphans, was a row of windows with the number 9 emblazoned on each of their shutters. The row was very long, stretching out to the left and right of the Baudelaires, so far that they couldn't see the end of it. Below this row of windows was another with the number 8 emblazoned on the shutters, and then another row with 7, and so on and so on, the numbers getting farther and farther away from the Baudelaires, all the way down to 0. Protruding from one of the 0 windows was a strange funnel, which was spewing a thick, white fog toward the siblings, covering a set of stairs leading to a large, curved archway one story above, marked ENTRANCE. The building was constructed from strange, shimmering bricks, and here and there on the building were large, strange flowers and patches of dark green moss, which all lay out on the ground in front of the children.

After a moment, one of the shutters opened, and in an instant the Baudelaires realized why the Hotel Denouement seemed so perplexing. They had not been staring at the building at all, but at its reflection in an enormous pond. The actual hotel stood at the far end of the pond, and was reflected onto the pond's surface. Normally, of course, it is easy to tell a building from its reflection in a body of water, but whoever had designed the Hotel Denouement had added several features to confuse passersby. For one thing, the building did not stand up straight, but tilted toward the ground at a precise angle, so that the pond only reflected the hotel, and none of the surrounding landscape and sky. Also, all of the hotel's signage—which is simply a fancy word meaning "signs"—was written backward, so the numbers on the windows could only be read correctly in the pond, and the words on the roof of the actual hotel read TИƎMƎUOИƎᗡ ⅃ƎTOH. Finally, some hard-working gardener had managed to grow lilies and moss on the bricks of the hotel—the same sort of lilies and moss that grow on the surface of ponds. The three siblings looked down at the pond, and then up at the hotel, back and forth several times, before they were able to get their bearings, a phrase which here means "stop staring at this perplexing sight and direct their attention to Kit Snicket."

"Over here, Baudelaires!" the pregnant woman called, and the children saw that Kit had taken a seat on an enormous blanket laid out on the lawn. The blanket was heaped with enough food to feed an army, had an army decided that morning to invade a pond. There were three loaves of bread, each baked into a different shape, lined up in front of little bowls of butter, jam, and what looked like melted chocolate. Alongside the bread was an enormous basket containing all sorts of pastries, from muffins to donuts to custard eclairs, which happened to be a favorite of Klaus's. There were two round tins containing quiche, which is a sort of pie made of eggs, cheese, and vegetables, and a large platter of smoked fish, and a wooden tray piled high with a pyramid of fruit. Three glass pitchers held three different kinds of juice, and there were silver pots containing coffee and tea, and laid out in a sort of fan was silverware with which to eat it all, and three napkins that were monogrammed, a word which here means "had the initials V. B., K. B., and S. B. embroidered on them."

"Sit down, sit down," Kit said, taking a bite of a pastry covered in powdered sugar. "As I said, we don't have much time, but that's no excuse for not eating well. Help yourselves to anything you like."

"Where did all this food come from?" Klaus asked.

"One of our associates laid it out for us," Kit said. "It is a policy of our organization that all picnics travel separately from the volunteers. If our enemies capture the picnic, they won't get their clutches on us, and if our enemies capture us, they won't get the picnic. That's something to remember during the next couple of days, as you participate in what one of our enemies calls the 'perpetual struggle for room and food.' Please try the marmalade. It's delicious."

The Baudelaires felt dizzy, as if their heads were still spinning from the ride through the shrubbery, and Violet reached into her pocket to find a ribbon. The conversation was so bewildering that the eldest Baudelaire wanted to concentrate as hard as she did when she was dreaming up an invention. Tying her hair up helped Violet focus her inventing mind, but before she could find a ribbon, Kit smiled kindly at her, and produced a ribbon of her own. She gestured for the eldest Baudelaire to sit down, and with a gentle look in her eyes, the distraught and pregnant woman tied Violet's hair up herself.

"You look just like your father." Kit sighed. "He wore the same frown whenever he was confused, although he almost never tied his hair up in a ribbon when he solved a problem. Please, Baudelaires, eat your brunch, and I'll try to catch you up on our current predicament. By the time you're eating your second pastry I hope your questions will be answered."

The Baudelaires sat down, spread their monogrammed napkins on their laps, and began to eat, surprised to find that they were just as hungry for brunch as they were curious for information. Violet took two slices of dark wheat bread and made herself a sandwich of smoked fish, deciding to try the chocolate spread afterward if she still had room. Klaus served himself some quiche and took a custard eclair, and Sunny rooted through the tray of fruit until she found a grapefruit, which she began to peel with her unusually sharp teeth. Kit smiled at the children, dabbed at her own mouth with a napkin embroidered with K. S., and began to speak.

"The building at the other end of the pond is the Hotel Denouement," she began. "Have you ever stayed there?"

"No," Violet said. "Our parents took us to the Hotel Preludio once for the weekend."

"That's right," Klaus said. "I'd almost forgotten."

"Carrots for breakfast," Sunny said, remembering the weekend with a smile.

"Well, the Hotel Preludio is a lovely place," Kit said, "but the Hotel Denouement is more than that. For years, it's been a place where our volunteers can gather to exchange information, discuss plans to defeat our enemies, and return books we've borrowed from one another. Before the schism, there were countless places that served such purposes. Bookstores and banks, restaurants and stationery stores, cafés and laundromats, opium dens and geodesic domes— people of nobility and integrity could gather nearly everywhere."

"Those must have been wonderful times," Violet said.

"So I'm told," Kit said. "I was four years old when everything changed. Our organization shattered, and it was as if the world shattered, too, and one by one the safe places were destroyed.

There was a large scientific laboratory, but the volunteer who owned the place was murdered. There was an enormous cavern, but a treacherous team of realtors claimed it for themselves. And there was an immense headquarters high in the Mortmain Mountains, but—"

"It was destroyed," Klaus said quietly. "We were there shortly after the fire."

"Of course you were," Kit said. "I'd forgotten. Well, the headquarters was the penultimate safe place."

"Penulhoo?" Sunny asked.

"'Penultimate' means 'next-to-last,'" Kit explained. "When the mountain headquarters was destroyed, only the Hotel Denouement was left. In every other place on Earth, nobility and integrity are vanishing quickly." She sighed, and gazed out at the still, flat surface of the pond. "If we're not careful, they'll vanish completely. Can you imagine a world in which wickedness and deception were running rampant?"

"Yes," Violet said quietly, and her siblings

nodded in agreement. They knew that the word "rampant" meant "without anyone to stop it," and they could imagine such a world very easily, because they had been living in one. Since their first encounter with Count Olaf, the villain's wickedness and deception had run rampant all over the Baudelaires' lives, and it had been very difficult for the children to keep from becoming villains themselves. In fact, when they considered all of their recent actions, they weren't entirely sure they hadn't performed a few acts of villainy, even if they'd had very good reasons for doing so.

"When we were in the mountains," Klaus said, "we found a message one of the volunteers had written. It said that V.F.D. would be gathering at the Hotel Denouement on Thursday."

Kit nodded, and reached to pour herself some more coffee. "Was the message addressed to J. S.?" she asked.

"Yes," Violet said. "We assumed the initials stood for Jacques Snicket."

"Brother?" Sunny asked.

Kit looked sadly down at her pastry. "Yes, Jacques was my brother. Because of the schism, I haven't seen either of my brothers for years, and it was only recently that I learned of his murder."

"We met Jacques very briefly," Violet said, referring to the time the Baudelaires had spent in the care of an entire village. "You must have been shocked to receive the news."

"Saddened," Kit said, "but not shocked. So many good people have been slain by our enemies." She reached across the blanket and patted the hands of all three Baudelaires in turn. "I know I don't have to tell you how terrible it feels to lose a family member. I felt so terrible that I vowed I would never leave my bed."

"What happened?" Klaus said.

Kit smiled. "I got hungry," she said, "and when I opened the refrigerator, I found another message waiting for me."

"Verbal Fridge Dialogue," Violet said, "the

same code as the message we found in the mountains."

"Yes," Kit said. "You three had been spotted by another volunteer. We knew, of course, that you children had nothing to do with my brother's death, no matter what that ridiculous reporter wrote in *The Daily Punctilio*."

The Baudelaires looked at one another. They had almost forgotten about Geraldine Julienne, a journalist who had caused them much inadvertent trouble, a phrase which here means "published in the newspaper that the Baudelaire orphans had murdered Jacques Snicket, whom she mistakenly identified as Count Olaf." The siblings had found it necessary to disguise themselves several times so as not to be captured by the authorities. "Who spotted us?" Klaus asked.

"Quigley Quagmire, of course," she said. "He found you in the Mortmain Mountains, and then managed to contact me when you were separated from him. He and I managed to meet each other in an abandoned bathrobe emporium, where we disguised ourselves as mannequins while we figured out what to do next. Finally, we managed to send a Volunteer Factual Dispatch to Captain Widdershins's submarine."

"*Queequeg*," Sunny said, naming the underwater vehicle where she and her siblings had recently spent a dreadful few days.

"Our plan was to meet up with you at Briny Beach," Kit said, "and proceed to the Hotel Denouement for the V.F.D. gathering."

"But where is Quigley?" Violet asked.

Kit sighed, and took a sip of her coffee. "He was very eager to see you," she said, "but he received word from his siblings."

"Duncan and Isadora!" Klaus cried. "We haven't seen them for quite some time. Are they safe?"

"I hope so," Kit answered. "The message they sent was incomplete, but it sounded as if they were being attacked in midair while flying over the sea. Quigley went to help them immediately in a helicopter we stole from a nearby botanist. If all goes well, you'll see all three Quagmire triplets on Thursday. That is, unless you cancel the gathering."

"Cancel it?" Violet asked. "Why would we do a thing like that?"

"The last safe place may not be safe after all," Kit said sadly. "If that's the case, you Baudelaires will need to send V.F.D. a signal that Thursday's gathering is canceled."

"Why not safe?" Sunny asked.

Kit smiled at the youngest Baudelaire, opened the cardboard folder that the Baudelaires had retrieved from the taxicab, and began to page through the papers inside. "I'm sorry this is so disorganized," she said. "I haven't had time to update my commonplace book. My brother used to say that if only one had a little more time to do some important reading, all the secrets in the world would become clear. I've scarcely looked at these maps, poems, and blueprints that Charles sent me, or chosen wallpaper for the baby's room. Wait one moment, Baudelaires. I'll find it."

The children helped themselves to more brunch, trying to be patient as Kit looked through her folder, pausing from time to time to smooth out the particularly crumpled papers. At last she held up a tiny piece of paper, no bigger than a caterpillar, which was rolled into a tiny scroll. "Here it is," she said. "A waiter slipped this to me last night by hiding it inside a cookie."

She handed it to Klaus, who unrolled the paper and squinted at it behind his glasses. "'J. S. has checked in,'" he read out loud, "'and requested tea with sugar. My brother sends his regards. Sincerely, Frank.'"

"Usually the messages inside the cookies are just superstitious nonsense," Kit said, "but recently the restaurant has changed management. You can understand why this message made me so distraught, Baudelaires. Someone is posing as my brother, and has checked into the hotel shortly before our entire organization is scheduled to arrive."

"Count Olaf," Violet said.

"It could be Olaf," Kit agreed, "but there are plenty of villains who are all too eager to be impostors. Those two villains in the mountains, for example."

"Or Hugo, Colette, or Kevin," Klaus said, naming three people the children had met at Caligari Carnival, who had since joined Olaf's troupe and had agreed to meet him at the hotel.

"But this J. S. isn't necessarily a wicked person," Kit said. "Plenty of noble people would check into the Hotel Denouement and order sugar in their tea. Not to sweeten it, of course— tea should be as bitter as wormwood, my brother used to say, and as sharp as a two-edged sword— but as a signal. Our comrades and our enemies are all after the same thing—the Vessel For Disaccharides."

"Sugar bowl," Sunny said, sharing a look of dismay with her siblings. The Baudelaires knew that Kit was referring to a sugar bowl that was of great importance to V.F.D. and to Count Olaf, who was desperate to get his hands on it. The children had searched for this sugar bowl from the highest peak of the Mortmain Mountains to the underwater depths of the Gorgonian Grotto, but had neither found this sugar bowl nor learned why it was so important.

"Exactly," Kit said. "The sugar bowl is on its way to the hotel even as we speak, and I'd hate to think what would happen if our enemies got ahold of it. I can't imagine anything worse, except perhaps if our enemies somehow got ahold of the Medusoid Mycelium."

The Baudelaires' look of dismay augmented, a word which here means "increased dramatically as they realized they had some bad news for Kit Snicket." "I'm afraid that Count Olaf has a small sample of the Medusoid Mycelium," Violet said, referring to a deadly fungus the children had encountered while exploring the ocean. Its sinister spores had infected poor Sunny, who might not have survived had her siblings not managed to dilute the poison in the nick of time. "We had a few spores locked tight in a diving helmet, but Olaf managed to steal it."

Kit gasped. "Then we most certainly have no time to lose. The three of you must infiltrate the Hotel Denouement and observe J. S. If J. S. is a noble person, then you must make sure that the sugar bowl falls into his or her hands, but if J. S. is a villainous person, you must make sure it does not. And I'm sad to say that this won't be as easy as it sounds."

"It doesn't sound easy at all," Klaus said.

"That's the spirit," Kit said, popping a grape into her mouth. "Of course, you won't be alone. Showing up early is one of the signs of a noble person, so there are other volunteers already at the hotel. You may even recognize some volunteers who have been observing you during your travels. But you also may recognize some of your enemies, as they will be posing as noble people by showing up early as well. While you try to observe the impostor, various impostors will undoubtedly be observing you."

"But how can we tell the volunteers from the enemies?" Violet asked.

"The same way you always do," Kit said. "When you first met Count Olaf, did you have any doubt he was a treacherous person? When you first met the Quagmire triplets, did you have any doubt that they were charming and resourceful? You'll have to observe everyone you see, and make such judgements yourselves. You Baudelaires will become flaneurs."

"Expound," Sunny said, which meant something along the lines of, "I'm afraid I don't know what that word means."

"Flaneurs," Kit explained, "are people who quietly observe their surroundings, intruding only when it is absolutely necessary. Children make excellent flaneurs, as so few people notice them. You'll be able to pass unnoticed in the hotel."

"We can't pass unnoticed," Klaus said. "*The*

Daily Punctilio has published our photographs in the paper. Someone is sure to recognize us and report our presence to the authorities."

"My brother's right," Violet said. "Three children just can't go wandering around a hotel observing things."

Kit smiled, and lifted one corner of the picnic blanket. Underneath were three parcels wrapped in paper. "The man who sent me the message about the impostor," she said, "is a member of V.F.D. He suggested that he hire the three of you as concierges. Your uniforms are in these packets."

"Expound again," Sunny said.

Klaus had taken out his commonplace book and was taking notes on what Kit was saying. The opportunity to define a word, however, was enough to interrupt his research. "A concierge," he said to his sister, "is someone who performs various tasks for guests in the hotel."

"It's the perfect disguise," Kit said. "You'll be doing everything from fetching packages to recommending restaurants. You'll be allowed in every corner of the hotel, from the rooftop sun-bathing salon to the laundry room in the basement, and no one will suspect you're there to spy on them. Frank will help you as best he can, but be very careful. The schism has turned many brothers into enemies. Under no circumstances should you reveal your true selves to Frank's treacherous identical brother Ernest."

"Identical?" Violet repeated. "If they're identical, how can we tell them apart?"

Kit took one last sip of her coffee. "Please try to pay attention," she said. "You'll have to observe everyone you see, and make such judgements yourselves. That's the only way to tell a villain from a volunteer. Now, is everything perfectly clear?"

The Baudelaires looked at one another. They could not remember a time in their lives when everything had been less clear than at this very moment, when every sentence Kit uttered seemed to be more mysterious than the last.

Klaus looked at the notes he had made in his commonplace book, and tried to summarize the errand Kit had outlined for them. "We're going to disguise ourselves as concierges," he said carefully, "in order to become flaneurs and observe an impostor who is either a volunteer or an enemy."

"A man named Frank is going to help us," Violet said, "but his brother Ernest will try to stop us."

"There are several other volunteers in the hotel," Klaus said, "but several other enemies as well."

"Sugar bowl," Sunny said.

"Very good," Kit said approvingly. "When you're done with your brunch, you can change into your uniforms behind that tree, and signal to Frank that you're on your way. Do you have something you can throw into the pond?"

Violet reached into her pocket and drew out a stone she had picked up on Briny Beach. "I imagine this will do," she said.

"That's perfect," Kit said. "Frank should be watching from one of the windows of the hotel, unless of course Ernest has intercepted my message and is watching instead. In any case, when you're ready to meet him, you can throw the rock into the pond, and he'll see the ripples and know you're on your way."

"Aren't you coming with us?" Klaus asked.

"I'm afraid not," Kit said. "I have other errands to perform. While Quigley tries to re-solve the situation in the sky, I will try to resolve the situation in the sea, and you'll have to resolve the situation here on land."

"Us alone?" Sunny asked. She meant something along the lines of, "Do you really think three children can accomplish all this by themselves?" and her siblings were quick to translate.

"Look at yourselves," Kit said, and gestured toward the pond. The Baudelaires stood up and stepped close to the water's edge, and leaned over the pond so their reflections appeared in front of the roof of the hotel. "When your parents died," Kit said, "you were just a young girl, Violet. But you've matured. Those aren't the eyes of a young girl. They're the eyes of someone who has faced endless hardship. And look at you, Klaus. You have the look of an experienced researcher—not just the young reader who lost his parents in a fire. And Sunny, you're standing on your own two feet, and so many of your teeth are growing in that they don't appear to be of such unusual size, as they were when you were a baby. You're not children anymore, Baudelaires. You're volunteers, ready to face the challenges of a desperate and perplexing world. You must go to the Hotel Denouement, and Quigley must go to the self-sustaining hot air mobile home, and I must go to a coral formation of dubious quality where an inflatable raft should be waiting. But if Quigley manages to construct a net big enough to capture all those eagles, and I manage to contact Captain Widdershins and have him meet me at a certain clump of seaweed, we'll be here on Thursday. Hector should manage to land his self-sustaining hot air mobile home on the roof, even with all of us aboard."

"Hector?" Violet said, remembering the man who had been so kind to them in the Village of Fowl Devotees, and his enormous invention that had carried him away from the Baudelaires. "He's safe?"

"I hope so," Kit said quietly, and stood up. She turned her face from the Baudelaires, and her voice seemed to tremble as she talked. "Don't worry about the brunch things, Baudelaires. One of my comrades has volunteered to clean up after our picnic. He's a wonderful gentleman. You'll meet him on Thursday, if all goes well. If all goes well—"

But she could not finish her sentence. Instead, she gave a little whimper, and her shoulders began to shake as the Baudelaires looked at one another. When someone is crying, of course, the noble thing to do is to comfort them. But if someone is trying to hide their tears, it may also be noble to pretend you do not notice them, so they will not be embarrassed. For a moment, the children could not choose between the noble activity of comforting a crying person and the noble activity of not embarrassing a crying person, but as Kit Snicket began to cry harder and harder they decided to comfort her. Violet clasped one of her hands. Klaus put an arm around her shoulder. Sunny hugged Kit above the knees, which was as high as she could reach.

"Why are you crying?" Violet asked. "Why are you so distraught?"

"Because all will not go well," Kit said finally. "You may as well know that now, Baudelaires. These are dark days, as dark as a crow flying through a pitch black night. Our errands may be noble, but we will not succeed. I suspect that before Thursday, I'll see your signal and know that all our hopes have gone up in smoke."

"But how will we signal?" Klaus asked.

"Which code should we use?"

"Any code you devise," Kit said. "We'll be watching the skies."

With that, she shook herself out of the children's comforting arms, and hurried away from the pond without another word to the siblings. Violet, Klaus, and Sunny watched her figure get smaller and smaller as she ran up the lawn, perhaps on her way back to the taxicab, or to join up with another mysterious volunteer, until at last she disappeared over the slope. For a moment none of the children said a word, and then Sunny reached down and picked up the parcels.

"Change?" she asked.

"I guess so," Violet said with a sigh. "It seems a shame to waste all this food, but I can't eat any more brunch."

"Perhaps the volunteer who is cleaning it up will bring it to someone else," Klaus said.

"Perhaps," Violet agreed. "There's so much about V.F.D. that remains a mystery."

"Perhaps we'll learn more when we're flâneurs," Klaus said. "If we observe everything around us, perhaps some of these mysteries will become clear. I hope so."

"I hope so, too," Violet said.

"Also hope so," Sunny said, and the Baudelaires said no more. Leaving their brunch behind, they ducked behind the tree Kit had suggested, and held up the picnic blanket as a sort of curtain, so each child could change into a concierge disguise in relative privacy. Violet buckled a shiny silver belt with the words HOTEL DENOUEMENT printed in large, black letters all the way around it, and hoped that she would be able to tell the difference between Frank and his treacherous brother Ernest. Klaus adjusted his stiff, round hat, which had a firm elastic band that tucked under the chin, and hoped he would know which of the guests were volunteers and which were villains. And Sunny slipped her fingers into the clean white gloves, surprised that Frank had managed to find them in such a small size, and hoped that she would be able to investigate the impostor posing as Jacques Snicket.

When the three children were all wearing their uniforms, they walked back to the edge of the pond and put on the last part of their disguises: three enormous pairs of sunglasses, reminding them of a disguise Count Olaf had worn when pretending to be a detective. The sunglasses were so large that they covered not only their eyes but a great portion of their faces—Klaus could even wear his regular glasses underneath them without anyone noticing. As they gazed through the sunglasses at their own reflections, they wondered if the disguises were enough to keep them out of the hands of the authorities long enough to solve all the mysteries that surrounded them, and they wondered if it was true what Kit Snicket had said, that they weren't children anymore, but volunteers ready to face the challenges of a desperate and perplexing world. The Baudelaires hoped so. But when Violet took the stone in her gloved hand, and threw it out into the middle of the pond, they wondered if their hopes would sink in the same way. They watched as the surface of the pond rippled, disrupting the reflection of the hotel. The children watched the shingles of the roof turn into a blur, and they watched the word "Denouement" disappear as if it were written on a piece of paper someone was crumpling in their hand. They watched each row of windows melt together, and they watched all the flowers and moss dissolve into nothing as the stone sank deeper and deeper into the pond, and the circular ripples spread further and further across the reflection. The Baudelaire orphans watched this reflected world disappear, and wondered if their hopes would also disappear, into the strange, rippling world of the Hotel Denouement and all the mysteries and secrets that lay deep inside.

Three

There are places where the world is quiet, but the enormous lobby of the Hotel Denouement was not one of them. On the day the Baudelaires walked up the stairs through the white fog from the funnel and entered the large, curved archway marked ƎƆИAЯTИƎ—or when reflected in the enormous pond, ENTRANCE—the lobby was bustling with activity. As Kit Snicket had predicted, the Baudelaires were able to pass unnoticed in the hotel, because everyone was far too busy to notice anything. Guests were lined up in front of a huge reception desk—which for some reason had the number 101 emblazoned on the wall above it—so they could check into the hotel and go to their rooms to freshen up. Bellboys and bellgirls were loading piles of luggage onto carts and rolling them toward the elevators—which for some reason had the number 118 emblazoned on their doors—so they could drop off the suitcases in the guests' rooms and collect their tips. Waiters and waitresses were bringing food and drink to people who were sitting on the chairs and benches of the lobby, waiting for refreshment. Taxi drivers were ushering guests into the lobby to join the line, and dogs were dragging their owners out of the lobby to take walks. Confused tourists were standing around looking quizzically at maps, and rambunctious children were playing hide-and-seek among the potted plants. A man in a tuxedo was sitting at a grand piano emblazoned with the number 152, playing tinkly tunes to amuse anyone who cared to listen, and members of the cleaning staff were discreetly polishing the green wooden floors etched with the number 123, for anyone who cared to see their feet reflected with every step. There was an enormous fountain in one corner of the room, releasing a cascade of water that ran over the number 131 in a shiny, smooth wall, and there was an enormous woman in the opposite corner, standing under the number 176 and shouting a man's name over and over in an increasingly annoyed tone of voice. The Baudelaires tried to be flaneurs as they walked across the chaos of the lobby, but there was so much to observe, and all of it was moving so quickly, that they wondered how they could even get started on their noble errand.

"I had no idea this place would be so busy," Violet said, blinking at the lobby from behind her sunglasses.

"How in the world will we be able to observe the impostor," Klaus wondered, "among all these possible suspects?"

"Frank first," Sunny said.

"Sunny's right," Violet said. "The first step

in our errand should be locating our new employer. If he saw our signal from that open window, he should be expecting us."

"Unless his villainous brother Ernest is expecting us instead," Klaus said.

"Or both," Sunny said.

"Why do you suppose there are so many numbers—" Violet started to ask, but before she could finish her question a man came bounding up to them. He was very tall and skinny, and his arms and legs stuck out at odd angles, as if he were made of drinking straws instead of flesh and bone. He was dressed in a uniform similar to that of the Baudelaires', but with the word MANAGER printed in fancy script over one of the pockets of his coat.

"You must be the new concierges," he said. "Welcome to the Hotel Denouement. I'm one of the managers."

"Frank," Violet asked, "or Ernest?"

"Exactly," the man said, and winked at them. "I'm so happy the three of you are here, even if one of you is unusually short, because we're unusually short-handed. I'm so busy you'll have to figure out the system for yourself."

"System?" Klaus asked.

"This place is as complicated as it is enormous," said Frank, or perhaps Ernest, "and vice versa. I'd hate to think what would happen if you didn't understand it."

The Baudelaires looked carefully at their new manager, but his face was utterly unfathomable, a word which here means "blank, so the Baudelaires could not tell if he was giving them a friendly warning or a sinister threat." "We'll try our best," Violet said quietly.

"Good," said the manager, leading the children across the enormous lobby. "You'll be at our guests' beck and call," he continued, using a phrase which meant that the guests would boss the Baudelaires around. "If anyone and everyone staying here asks for assistance, you'll immediately volunteer to help them."

"Excuse me, sir," interrupted one of the

bellboys. He was holding a suitcase in each hand and wearing a confused expression on his face. "This luggage arrived in a taxi, but the driver said the guest wouldn't arrive until Thursday. What should I do?"

"Thursday?" said Frank or Ernest with a frown. "Excuse me, concierges. I don't suppose I have to tell you how important this is. I'll be right back."

The manager followed the bellboy into the crowd, leaving the Baudelaires standing alone next to a large, wooden bench marked with the number 128. Klaus ran his hand along the bench, which was etched with rings, from people setting down glasses without using coasters. "Do you think we were talking to Frank," Klaus said, "or Ernest?"

"I don't know," Violet said. "He used the word 'volunteer.' Maybe that was some sort of a code."

"Thursinterest," Sunny said, which meant "He knew that Thursday was important."

"That's true," Klaus said, "but is it important to him because he's a volunteer or a villain?"

Before either Baudelaire sister could hazard a guess, a phrase which here means "attempt to answer Klaus's question," the tall, skinny manager reappeared at their sides. "You must be the new concierges," he said, and the children realized that this was the other brother. "Welcome to the Hotel Denouement."

"You must be Ernest," Violet tried.

"Or Frank," Sunny said.

"Yes," the manager said, although it was not at all clear with whom he was agreeing. "I'm very grateful you three are here. The hotel is quite busy at the moment, and we're expecting more guests to arrive on Thursday. Now, you'll be stationed at the concierge desk, number 175, right over here. Follow me."

The children followed him to the far wall of the lobby, where a large wooden desk sat under the number 175, which was painted over an enormous window. On the desk was a small lamp shaped like a frog, and out the window, the children could see the gray, flat horizon of the sea. "We've got a pond on one side of us," said Ernest, unless of course it was Frank, "and the sea on the other side. It doesn't sound very safe, and yet some people think this is a very safe place indeed." Frank, unless it was Ernest, looked around hurriedly and lowered his voice. "What do you think?"

Once again, the manager's face was unfathomable, and the children could not tell if his reference to a safe place made him a volunteer or a villain. "Hmm," Sunny said, which is often a safe answer, even though it is not really an answer at all.

"Hmm," Frank or Ernest said in response. "Now then, let me explain how this hotel is organized."

"Excuse me, sir," said a bellgirl, whose face could not be seen behind the pile of newspapers she was carrying. "The latest edition of *The Daily Punctilio* has arrived."

"Let me see," said either Ernest or Frank, plucking a copy from the top of the pile. "I heard that Geraldine Julienne has written an update on the Baudelaire case."

The Baudelaire orphans froze, scarcely daring to look at one another, let alone the volunteer or villain who was standing beside them reading the headline out loud. "'BAUDELAIRES RUMORED TO RETURN TO THE CITY,'" he said. "'According to information recently discovered by this reporter when opening a cookie, Veronica, Klyde, and Susie Baudelaire, the notorious murderers of renowned actor Count Omar, are returning to the city, perhaps to commit more vicious murders or to continue their recent hobby of arson. Citizens are advised to watch for these three bloodthirsty children, and to report them to the authorities if they are spotted. If they are not spotted, citizens are advised to do nothing.'" The manager turned to the Baudelaires, his face as unfathomable as ever. "What do you think of that, concierges?"

"That's an interesting question," Klaus replied, which is another very safe answer.

"I'm glad you find it interesting," Ernest or Frank replied, which was an equally safe answer to Klaus's safe answer. Then he turned to the bellgirl. "I'll show you the newsstand in Room 168," he said, and disappeared with the newspapers into the crowd, leaving the Baudelaires alone, standing at the desk and staring out to sea.

"I think that was Ernest," Violet said. "His comment about the hotel's safety sounded very sinister."

"But he didn't seem alarmed by the story in *The Daily Punctilio*," Klaus said. "If Ernest is an enemy of V.F.D., he'd be on the watch for us. So that man was probably Frank."

"Maybe he just didn't recognize us," Violet said. "After all, few people recognize Count Olaf when he's in disguise, and his disguises aren't much better than ours. Maybe we look more like concierges than Baudelaires."

"Or maybe we don't look like Baudelaires at

all," Klaus said. "As Kit said, we're not children anymore."

"Nidiculous," Sunny said, which meant something like, "I think I'm still a child."

"That's true," Klaus admitted, smiling down at his sister, "but the older we get, the less likely it is that we'll be recognized."

"That should make it easier to do our errands," Violet said.

"What do you mean by that?" asked a familiar voice, and the Baudelaires saw that either Frank or Ernest had returned.

"What my associate meant," Klaus said, thinking quickly, "is that it would be easier for us to start our work as concierges if you explained how the hotel is organized."

"I just said I would do that," said Frank in an annoyed voice, or Ernest in an irritated one. "Once you understand how the Hotel Denouement works, you'll be able to perform your errands as easily as you would find a book in a library. And if you can find a book in a library, then you already know how this hotel works."

"Expound," Sunny said.

"The Hotel Denouement is organized according to the Dewey Decimal System," Frank or Ernest explained. "That's the same way books are organized in many libraries. For instance, if you wanted to find a book on German poetry, you would begin in the section of the library marked 800, which contains books on literature and rhetoric. Similarly, the eighth story of this hotel is reserved for our rhetorical guests. Within the 800 section of a library, you'd find books on German poetry labeled 831, and if you were to take the elevator up to the eighth story and walk into Room 831, you'd find a gathering of German poets. Understand?"

"I think so," said Klaus. All three Baudelaires had spent enough time in libraries to be familiar with the Dewey Decimal System, but even Klaus's vast experience in research did not mean he had committed the entire system to memory. It is not necessary, of course, to

memorize the Dewey Decimal System in order
to use a library, as most libraries have catalogs,
in which all of the books are listed on cards or
on a computer screen to make them easier to
find. "Where can we find the catalog for the
Hotel Denouement's services?"

"Catalog?" repeated either Frank or Ernest.
"You shouldn't need a catalog. The entire 100
section of a library is dedicated to philosophy
and psychology, and so is the first story of our
hotel, from the reception desk, which is labeled
101 for the theory of philosophy, to the concierge desk, which is labeled 175 for the ethics
of recreation and leisure, to the couches over
there, which are labeled 135, for dreams and
mysteries, in case our guests want to take a nap
or conceal something underneath the sofa cushions. The second story is the 200s, for religion,
and we have a church, a cathedral, a chapel,
a synagogue, a mosque, a temple, a shrine, a
shuffleboard court, and Room 296, which is cur-
rently occupied by a somewhat cranky rabbi.

The third story is the social sciences, where we have placed our ballrooms and meeting rooms; the fourth story is dedicated to language, so most of our foreigners stay there. The 500s are dedicated to mathematics and science, and the sixth story is dedicated to technology, from the sauna in Room 613, which stands for the promotion of health, to Room 697, which is where we keep the controls for heating, ventilation, and air conditioning. Now, if the seventh story stands for the arts, what do you think we would find in Room 792, which stands for stage presentations?"

Violet wanted to tie her hair up in a ribbon to help her think, but she was afraid of being recognized. "A theater?" she said.

"You've obviously visited a library before," the manager said, although the children could not tell if he was complimenting them or getting suspicious. "I'm afraid that's not true of all of our guests, so when they are in need of any of our services, they ring for a concierge instead of wandering around the hotel by themselves. In the next day or so, you'll probably walk through every section of the hotel, from the astronomy observatory in Room 999 to the employees' quarters in the basement, Room 000."

"Is that where we sleep?" Klaus asked.

"Well, you're on duty twenty-four hours a day," Ernest said, or perhaps it was Frank. "But the hotel gets very quiet at night, when the guests go to sleep, or stay up all night reading. You can nap behind the desk, and when someone rings for you it will serve as an alarm clock."

Frank stopped talking, or perhaps it was Ernest, and quickly looked around the room before leaning in close to the Baudelaires. The three siblings nervously looked back at Ernest through their sunglasses, or maybe it was Frank. "Your positions as concierges," he said in his unfathomable tone, "are excellent opportunities for you to quietly observe your surroundings. People tend to treat the hotel staff as if they are invisible, so you will have the chance to see and hear quite a lot of interesting things. However, you should remember that you will also have many opportunities to be observed. Do I make myself clear?"

This time it was Violet who needed to give a safe answer. "Hmm," she said. "That's an interesting question."

Either Frank or Ernest narrowed his eyes at the oldest Baudelaire, and seemed about to say something when the Baudelaires suddenly heard some loud, piercing ringing sounds. "Aha!" the manager cried. "Your work has begun!"

The siblings followed Ernest or Frank around to the other side of the desk, and Frank or Ernest pointed to a vast network of tiny bells, each no larger than a thimble, which lined the back of a desk where knobs for drawers might otherwise be. Each bell had a number on it, from 000 to 999, with one extra bell that had no number at all. This extra bell was ringing, along with the bell numbered 371 and the bell numbered 674.

"Ring!" cried either Ernest or Frank. "Ring! I shouldn't have to tell you the bell's your signal. We can't keep our guests waiting for even an instant. You can tell which guest is ringing by the number on the bell. If the number written on the bell was 469, for example, you would know that one of our Portuguese guests required assistance. Are you paying attention? The bell marked 674 indicates our associates in the lumber industry, as the number 674 means lumber processing or wood products in the Dewey Decimal System. We can't make enemies out of important guests! The number 371 indicates educational guests. Please be nice to them, too, although they're much less important. Respond to all of our guests whenever you hear that ring!"

"But what does that unmarked bell refer to?" Klaus asked. "The Dewey Decimal System doesn't go higher than 999."

The manager frowned, as if the middle Baudelaire had given him the wrong answer.

"That's the rooftop sunbathing salon," he said. "People who sunbathe aren't usually interested in library science, so they're not picky about the salon's location. Now, get moving!"

"But where shall we go first?" Violet said. "Guests have requested assistance in three places at once."

"You'll have to split up, of course," Frank or Ernest replied, as unfathomably as ever. "Each concierge will choose a guest and hurry to their location. Take the elevators—they're at 118, for force and energy."

"Excuse me, sir," said another bellboy, tapping Ernest or Frank on the shoulder. "There's a banker on the phone who wants to speak to one of the managers right away."

"I'd better get to work," the manager said, "and so should you, concierges. Off with you!"

"Off with you" is a phrase used by people who lack the courtesy to say something more polite, such as "If there's nothing else you require, I must be going," or "I'm sorry, but I'm going to have to ask you to leave, please," or even "Excuse me, but I believe you have mistaken my home for your own, and my valuable belongings for yours, and I must ask you to return the items in question to me, and leave my home, after untying me from this chair, as I am unable to do it myself, if it's not too much trouble." The children were not pleased to be dismissed so rudely, nor were they pleased to learn that their employment as concierges would involve such a complicated organizational method in an immense and confusing hotel. They were not pleased that they had not been able to discern which manager was Frank and which was Ernest, and they were not pleased to learn that *The Daily Punctilio* was alerting the city's citizens to the Baudelaires' arrival, and that someone might recognize them at any moment and have them arrested for crimes they had not committed. But most of all, the Baudelaires were not pleased by the notion of splitting up and doing separate errands in this perplexing hotel. They had hoped to perform their duties as concierges and flaneurs together, and with each step toward the elevators they grew more and more unhappy at the idea of leaving one another behind.

"I'll go to the rooftop sunbathing salon," Violet said, trying to be brave. "Klaus, why don't you take Room 674, and Sunny, you can take Room 371. We'll all meet up at the concierge desk when we're done."

"We'll be able to observe more this way," Klaus said hopefully. "With the three of us on three separate stories, we can find the impostor much more quickly."

"Unsafe," Sunny said, which meant something along the lines of, "I'd rather not find the impostor if I'm all by myself."

"You'll be safe, Sunny," Klaus said. "This hotel is just like a large library."

"Yes," Violet said. "And what's the worst thing that can happen in a library?"

The two younger Baudelaires did not answer her, and the three concierges stood in silence for a few moments, gazing at a small sign posted near the elevators' sliding doors. When one pair of doors finally opened, the children stepped inside and pressed the appropriate buttons for their guests' locations, and as the small elevator began to rise, the children remembered the elevator shaft at 667 Dark Avenue, which it had been necessary to climb up and down several times. The Baudelaires had learned the worst thing that could happen in an elevator shaft, which was being thrown down one by a villainous girlfriend. The Baudelaires had learned the worst thing that could happen at a lumbermill, which was being forced to cause a violent accident through the sinister power of hypnotism. And the Baudelaires had learned the worst thing that could happen at a school, which was meeting some dear friends, only to have them dragged away in a long, black automobile. The orphans learned what the worst thing was at a herpetologist's house, and what the worst thing was in a small town, and at a hospital, and at a carnival, and at the peak of a mountaintop, and in a submarine, and a cave, and within the currents of a rushing stream, and inside the trunk of a car and in a pit full of lions and in a secret passageway and many, many other sinister places they preferred not to think about at all, and throughout all these perils they had encountered, and the countless other perils besides, they had always found a library of some sort or another, where the children managed to discover the crucial information necessary to save their skins, a phrase which here means "keep them alive for the next terrible chapter in their lives." But now the Baudelaires' new home was a library—a strange one, of course, but a library nonetheless—and as the elevator took them silently through the library toward their separate destinations, they did not like to wonder what the worst thing was that could happen at a library, particularly after reading the first four words on the small, posted sign. IN CASE OF FIRE, the sign read, and as the Baudelaire orphans went their separate ways, they did not like to think of that at all.

NOT A CHAPTER

As I'm sure you've noticed, most of the history of the Baudelaire orphans is organized sequentially, a word which here means "so that the events in the lives of Violet, Klaus, and Sunny Baudelaire are related in the order in which they occurred." In the case of the next three chapters, however, the story is organized simultaneously, which means that you do not have to read the chapters in the order in which they appear. In chapter four, you may find the story of Violet Baudelaire's journey up to the rooftop sunbathing salon, and the unpleasant conversation she had occasion to overhear. In chapter five, you may read about Klaus's experience with certain members of the lumber industry, and a sinister plot that was devised right in front of his nose. And in chapter six, you may see the result of my research into Sunny's dreadful visit to Room 371 and to a mysterious restaurant located on the ninth story. But because all of them occur at the very same time, you need not read the chapters in the sequence four-five-six, but can read them in any order you choose. Or, more sensibly, you could simply skip all three chapters, along with the seven chapters that follow them, and find some other sequential or simultaneous thing with which to occupy your time.

CHAPTER Four

When the elevator finally reached the roof, and the doors slid open to allow her to exit, Violet Baudelaire had two reasons to be grateful that her concierge disguise included sunglasses. For one thing, the rooftop sunbathing salon was very, very bright. The morning fog, so thick when the Baudelaires arrived on Briny Beach, had disappeared, and the rays of the afternoon sun beat down on the entire city, reflecting off every shiny object, from the glistening waters of the sea, which splashed against the opposite side of the hotel, to the surface of the pond, which had settled since Violet had thrown the stone. All along the edge of the roof were large, rectangular mirrors, tilted like the hotel itself, catching the blinding light of the afternoon sun and bouncing it onto the skin of the sunbathing guests. Ten sunbathers, their bare skin coated in thick, sticky lotion, lay without moving on shiny mats arranged around a heated swimming pool, which was so warm that clouds of steam were floating up from the surface. In a corner was an attendant, his eyes covered in green sunglasses and his body covered in a long, baggy robe. He was holding two enormous spatulas, such as might be used to flip pancakes, and from time to time he would reach out with a spatula and flip over one of the sunbathers, so that their bellies and backs would be the same shade of brown. The spatulas, like the mirrors and the mats and the pool, reflected the light of the sun, and Violet was glad her eyes were shielded.

But there was another reason the eldest Baudelaire was grateful for the sunglasses, and it had to do with the person who was waiting impatiently by the doors to the elevator. This person was also wearing sunglasses, although these were much more unusual. Instead of lenses, there were two large cones sticking out from the eyes, getting wider and wider until they stopped, as wide as dinner plates, several feet in front of the person's face. Such a pair of glasses might have concealed the identity of the person who was wearing them, but they were so ridiculous that Violet knew there could be only one person so obsessed with being fashionable that she would wear such ridiculous eyewear, and Violet was grateful that her own identity was concealed.

"Here you are at last," said Esmé Squalor. "I thought I'd never see you here."

"Pardon me?" Violet asked nervously.

"Are you deaf, concierge?" Esmé demanded. Her scornful frown was lined with silver lipstick, as if she had been drinking molten metal, and she pointed an accusing finger with a long, silver nail. The nails had been filed into individual shapes, so that each hand spelled "E-S-M-É," with the thumbnail carved into the familiar symbol of an eye. The letters were painted to match Esmé's sandals, which had long, frilly straps that ran around and around the notorious girlfriend's bare legs like centipedes. The rest of Esmé's outfit, I regret to say, consisted of three large leaves of lettuce, attached to her body with tape. If you have ever seen the bathing garment known as the bikini, then you can guess where these pieces of lettuce were attached, and if you cannot guess then I advise you to ask someone of your acquaintance who is not as squeamish as I am about discussing the bodies of villainous women. "Glamorous people like myself don't have time to be nice to the deaf," she snarled. "I rang the concierge bell more than two minutes ago, and I've been wait-ing the entire time!"

"I can see the headline now," crowed another voice. "'UNBELIEVABLY GLAMOROUS AND BEAUTIFUL WOMAN COMPLAINS ABOUT HOTEL SERVICE!' Wait until the readers of *The Daily Punctilio* see that!"

Violet was so relieved not to be recognized that she hadn't noticed who was standing next to Count Olaf's treacherous girlfriend. Geraldine Julienne was the irresponsible journalist who had printed so many lies about the Baudelaires, and she wasn't happy to see that the reporter had become one of Esmé's sycophants, a word which here means "people who enjoy flattering people who enjoy being flattered."

"I'm sorry, ma'am," Violet said, in as pro-fessional a tone as she could muster. "The concierges are particularly busy today. What is it you require?"

"It's not what *I* require," Esmé said, "it's what the adorable little girl in the pool requires."

"I'm not an adorable little girl!" Yet another familiar voice came from the direction of the heated pool, and Violet turned to see Carmelita Spats, a spoiled and unpleasant child the Baudelaires had first encountered at boarding school, who had gone on to join Count Olaf and Esmé Squalor in performing treacherous deeds. "I'm a ballplaying cowboy superhero soldier pirate!" she cried, emerging from a cloud of steam. She was wearing an outfit as ridiculous as Esmé's, though thankfully it wasn't as revealing. She had on a bright blue jacket, covered with shiny medals such as are given to people for military service, which was unbuttoned to reveal a white shirt that proclaimed the name of a sports team in curly blue letters. Stapled to the back of her jacket was a long, blue cape, and on her feet were a pair of bright blue boots with spurs, which are tiny wheels of spikes used to urge animals to move more quickly than they might otherwise prefer. She had a blue patch covering one of her eyes, and on her head was a blue triangular hat with a skull and crossbones printed on it—the symbol that pirates use while prowling the high seas. Carmelita Spats, of course, was not on the high seas, but had managed to drag a large, wooden boat to the rooftop sunbathing salon so she could prowl a high swimming pool. On the bow of the boat was an ornately carved figurehead, a word which here means "wooden statue of an octopus attacking a man in a diving suit," and there was a tall mast, stretching up toward the sky, which held a billowing sail that had the insignia of an eye matching the one on Count Olaf's ankle. The eldest Baudelaire stared for a moment at this hideous figurehead, but then turned her attention to Carmelita. The last time Violet had seen the unpleasant captain of this boat, she was dressed all in pink, and was announcing herself as a tap-dancing ballerina fairy princess veterinarian, but the eldest Baudelaire could hardly say whether being a ballplaying cowboy superhero soldier pirate was better or worse.

"Of course you are, darling," purred Esmé,

and turned to Geraldine Julienne with a smile one mother might give another at a playground. "Carmelita has been a tomboy lately," she said, using an insulting term inflicted on girls whose behavior some people find unusual.

"I'm sure your daughter will grow out of it," Geraldine replied, who as usual was speaking into a microphone.

"Carmelita Spats is not my daughter," Esmé said haughtily. "I'd no sooner have children of my own than I would wear modest clothing."

"I thought you adopted three orphans," Geraldine said.

"When it was in," Esmé hurriedly added, using her usual word for "fashionable." "But orphans are out now."

"Then what's in?" asked Geraldine breathlessly.

"Planning cocktail parties in hotels, of course!" crowed Esmé. "Why else would I let a ridiculous woman like yourself interview me?"

"How wonderful!" cried Geraldine, who

appeared not to realize she had just been insulted. "I can see the headline now: 'ESMÉ SQUALOR, THE MOST GLAMOROUS PERSON EVER!' Wait until the readers of *The Daily Punctilio* see that! When they read about your career as an actress, financial advisor, girlfriend, and cocktail party hostess, they'll get so excited that some of them will probably have heart attacks!"

"I hope so," Esmé said.

"I'm sure my readers will want to know all about your stylish outfit," Geraldine said, holding her microphone under Esmé's chin. "Will you tell us something about those unusual glasses you're wearing?"

"They're sunoculars," Esmé said, patting her strange eyewear. "They're a combination of sunglasses and binoculars. They're very in, and this way I can watch the skies without getting the sun in my eyes—or the moon, if something should happen to arrive at night."

"Why would you want to watch the skies?" Geraldine asked curiously.

Esmé frowned, and Violet could tell that the stylish woman had let something slip, a phrase which here means "said something she wished she hadn't." "Because birdwatching is very in," she said unconvincingly, a word which here means "clearly telling a lie."

"Wait until the readers of *The Daily Punctilio* hear that!" gasped Geraldine. "Will all the guests at your cocktail party be wearing sunoculars?"

"No matter what the guests are wearing," Esmé said with a smirk, "they won't be able to see the surprises we have in store for them."

"What surprises?" Geraldine asked eagerly.

"If I told you what they were," Esmé said, "they wouldn't be surprises."

"Couldn't you give me a hint?" Geraldine asked.

"No," Esmé said.

"Not even a little one?" Geraldine asked.

"No," Esmé said.

"Pretty please?" Geraldine whined. "Pretty please with sugar on top?"

Esmé's silver-coated lips curled thoughtfully. "If I give you a hint," she said, "you'll
have to tell me something, too. You're a reporter,
so you know all sorts of interesting information.
Before I reveal my special hors d'oeuvres for
Thursday's cocktail party, I want you to tell me
something about a certain guest at this hotel.
He's been lurking around the basement, plot-
ting to spoil our party. His initials are J. S."

"Lurking around the basement?" Geraldine
repeated. "But J. S. is—"

"Esmé!" Carmelita screamed from the
swimming pool, interrupting at just the worst
moment. "That concierge is just standing there,
when she's supposed to be at my beck and call!
She's nothing but a cakesniffer!"

Esmé turned to Violet, who was used to
being called a cakesniffer after all this time.
"What are you waiting for?" she snarled. "Go
get whatever that darling little girl wants!"

Esmé twirled around and marched away,
and Violet was glad to see that the villainous

girlfriend's outfit had two more lettuce leaves than had been visible from the front. The eldest Baudelaire was sorry to stop performing her flaneur errands and begin her duties as a concierge, but she stepped to the edge of the swimming pool, walking carefully on the tilted roof of the hotel and peering into the clouds of steam. "What is it you want, miss?" she asked, hoping Carmelita would not recognize her voice.

"A harpoon gun, of course!" Carmelita said. "Countie said that I can't be a ballplaying cowboy superhero soldier pirate without a harpoon gun."

"Who's Countie?" Geraldine asked.

"Esmé's boyfriend," Carmelita said. "He thinks I'm the most darling, special little girl in the entire world. He said if I used my harpoon gun properly he would teach me how to spit like a real ballplaying cowboy superhero soldier pirate!"

"I can see the headline now," Geraldine said into her microphone. "'BALLPLAYING COWBOY

SUPERHERO SOLDIER PIRATE LEARNS TO SPIT!'
Wait until the readers of *The Daily Punctilio* see
that!"

"I'll fetch you a harpoon gun, miss." Violet
promised, ducking to avoid the attendant's spatula, which was overturning a sunbathing woman.

"Stop calling me 'miss,' you cakesniffer!"
Carmelita said. "I'm a ballplaying cowboy
superhero soldier pirate!"

Fetching objects for people who are too lazy
to fetch them for themselves is never a pleasant
task, particularly when the people are insulting
you, but as Violet walked back to the elevator and
pressed the button for it to arrive, she was not
thinking about Carmelita's atrocious behavior.
She was too preoccupied, a word which here
means "wondering what exactly Esmé Squalor
and Carmelita Spats were doing at the Hotel
Denouement." The two unsavory females knew
full well about V.F.D. and the plans for Thursday's gathering, but the eldest Baudelaire did not
believe for a minute that all they were planning

was a cocktail party. As the doors slid open and Violet stepped inside, she wondered why Esmé was using her sunoculars to search the skies. She wondered what Carmelita wanted with a harpoon gun. She wondered how Esmé knew about the impostor J. S., who was apparently lurking around the basement of the hotel. But most of all, she wondered where Count Olaf—or, as Carmelita liked to call him, "Countie"—was hiding, and what treachery he was planning.

Violet was thinking so hard about her observations as a flaneur that it was only when the elevator doors shut that she remembered her errand as a concierge, and realized that she had no idea where to find a harpoon gun. Harpoon guns are not part of the usual equipment provided by a hotel, and the only time Violet had seen such a device was in Esmé Squalor's own hands, back when she was disguised as a policewoman at the Village of Fowl Devotees. Even if the Hotel Denouement had thought to keep such a thing in the building, Violet could not imagine where she might find it in the Dewey Decimal System without a catalog. She wished Klaus were with her, as the only number of the Dewey Decimal System she knew by heart was 621, which labeled her favorite section, applied physics. With a glum sigh, the eldest Baudelaire pressed the button for the lobby.

"You're asking me for help?" cried either Frank or Ernest, when Violet managed to find him. The lobby of the Hotel Denouement was even more crowded than when the Baudelaires had arrived, and it took Violet a few minutes before she could find the familiar figure of the volunteer or his villainous brother. "I'm the one who needs help," he said. "An astonishing number of guests have arrived earlier than expected. I have no time to be a concierge helper."

"I realize that you're busy, sir," Violet said. She knew that calling a person "sir" can often help you get what you want, unless of course the person is a woman. "A guest has requested a harpoon gun, and I don't know where to find one.

I wish the Hotel Denouement had a catalog."

"You shouldn't need a catalog," the manager said. "Not if you're who I think you are."

Violet gasped, and either Frank or Ernest took one step closer to her. "Are you?" he asked. "Are you who I think you are?"

Violet blinked behind her sunglasses. There are people in this world who say that silence is golden, which simply means that they prefer a calm and peaceful hush to the noise and clutter of the world. There is nothing wrong with such a preference, but sadly there are times when a calm and peaceful hush is simply not possible. If you are watching the sun set, for instance, silence may permit you to be alone with your thoughts as you gaze at the darkening landscape, but it may be necessary to make a loud noise to scare off any grizzly bears that may be approaching. If you are riding in a taxi, you might prefer silence so you can study your map in peace, but the occasion may require you to shout, "Please turn around!

I think they've driven through those hedges!" And if you have lost a loved one, as the Baudelaires did on the fateful day of a fire, you may wish very dearly for a long period of silence, so you and your siblings can contemplate your puzzling and woeful situation, but you may find yourself tossed from one dangerous situation to another, and another, and another, so that you begin to think you will never find yourself in a calm and peaceful hush. As Violet stood in the lobby, she wanted nothing more than to be silent, so that she might further observe the man standing next to her, and discover if he was a volunteer, to whom she could say, "Yes, I'm Violet Baudelaire," or a villain, to whom she could say, "I'm sorry; I don't know what you're talking about." But she knew that she could not not hope for a calm and peaceful hush in the chaos of Hotel Denouement, and so rather than remain silent she answered the manager's question as best she could.

"Of course I'm who you think I am," she

said, feeling as if she were talking in code, although in a code she did not know. "I'm a concierge."

"I see," said Frank or Ernest unfathomably. "And who is requesting the harpoon gun?"

"A young girl on the roof," Violet said.

"A young girl on the roof," the manager repeated with a sly smile. "Are you sure a harpoon gun should be given to a young girl on the roof?"

Violet did not know how to answer him, but fortunately this appeared to be one of the times when silence is in fact golden, because at her silence, Frank or Ernest gave the eldest Baudelaire another smile and then turned on his heel—a phrase which here means "turned around in a somewhat fancy manner"—and beckoned Violet to follow him to a far corner of the lobby, where she saw a small door marked 121. "This number stands for epistemology," he explained, using a word which here means "theories of knowledge" and looking hurriedly around the lobby as if he were being watched. "I thought it would be a good hiding place."

Frank or Ernest took a key out of his pocket and unlocked the door, which swung open with a quiet creak to reveal a small, bare closet. The only thing in the closet was a large, wicked-looking object, with a bright red trigger and four long, sharp hooks. The eldest Baudelaire recognized it from her stay in the Village of Fowl Devotees. She knew it was a harpoon gun, a deadly device that ought not to be in the hands of anyone, let alone Carmelita Spats. Violet did not want to touch it herself, but as the manager stood at the door gazing at her, she could think of no other choice, and carefully removed the device from the closet.

"Be very careful with this," the manager said in an unfathomable tone. "A weapon like this should only be in the hands of the right person. I'm grateful for your assistance, concierge. Not many people have the courage to help with a scheme like this."

Violet nodded silently, and silently took the heavy weapon from Frank or Ernest's hands. In silence she walked back to the elevators, her head spinning with her mysterious observations as a flaneur and her mysterious errand as a concierge, and in silence she stood at the sliding elevator doors, wondering which manager she had spoken to, and what precisely she had said to him in her coded, quiet response. But just before the elevator arrived, Violet's silence was shattered by an enormous noise.

The clock in the lobby of the Hotel Denouement is the stuff of legend, a phrase which here means "very famous for being very loud." It is located in the very center of the ceiling, at the very top of the dome, and when the clock announces the hour, its bells clang throughout the entire building, making an immense, deep noise that sounds like a certain word being uttered once for each hour. At this particular moment, it was three o'clock, and everyone in the hotel could hear the booming ring of the enormous bells of the clock, uttering the word three times in succession: *Wrong! Wrong! Wrong!*

As she boarded the elevator, the harpoon gun heavy and sinister in her gloved hands, Violet Baudelaire felt as if the clock were scolding her for her efforts at solving the mysteries of the Hotel Denouement. *Wrong!* She had tried her best to be a flaneur, but hadn't observed enough to decode the scheme of Esmé Squalor and Carmelita Spats. *Wrong!* She had tried to communicate with one of the hotel's managers, but had been unable to discover whether he was Frank or Ernest. And—most *Wrong!* of all— she was now taking a deadly weapon to the rooftop sunbathing salon, where it would serve some unknown, sinister purpose. With each strike of the clock, Violet felt wronger and wronger, until at last she reached her destination, and stepped out of the elevator. She dearly hoped her two siblings had found more success in their errands, for as she walked across the roof, avoiding a spatula as it flipped the guests on their mirrored mats, until at last she could hoist the harpoon gun into Carmelita's eager and ungrateful hands, all the eldest Baudelaire could think was that everything was wrong, wrong, wrong.

CHAPTER
Five

When the elevator
reached the sixth story,
Klaus bade good-bye to Violet and
stepped out into a long, empty hallway.
The hallway was lined with numbered
doors, odd numbers on one side and even
numbers on the other, and large ornamental vases, too large to hold flowers
and too small to hold spies. On the floor
was a smooth, gray carpet that muffled
each of the middle Baudelaire's
uncertain steps. Although Klaus
had never set foot

in the Hotel Denouement before today, walking down the hallway gave him a familiar feeling. It was the feeling he had whenever he entered a library with an important problem to solve, suspecting that somewhere within the library's collection of books was the perfect answer to whatever question was foremost on his mind. He had this feeling when he and his siblings were living just off Lousy Lane, and he solved the murder of Uncle Monty with crucial information he discovered in a herpetological library. He had this feeling when he and his siblings were deep in the ocean, and he managed to dilute the poison infecting Sunny by finding a significant fact in a mycological library belonging to Fiona, a young woman who had broken Klaus's heart. And as he stood in the hallway, gazing at all of the numbered doors that stretched out as far as his eyes could see, Klaus Baudelaire had the feeling again. Hidden somewhere in this hotel, he was sure, was something or someone that could answer all the Baudelaires' questions, solve all of the Baudelaires' mysteries, and put an end at last to all the Baudelaires' woes. It was as if he could hear this answer calling to him, like a baby crying at the bottom of a damp well, or an alarm clock ringing underneath a heap of damp blankets.

Without a catalog, however, Klaus had no idea where such a solution might be, so he made his way toward his concierge errand in Room 674, hoping that whatever he would observe as a flaneur might bring him closer to unraveling the Baudelaires' list of misfortunes. When he stopped in front of the numbered door, how-ever, it appeared that he was only adding another misfortune to this woeful list. Smoke was pouring out of the gap between the door and the floor, spreading out across the hallway like a sinister stain.

"Hello?" Klaus called, knocking on the door.

"Hello yourself," called back a voice that sounded slightly familiar and utterly uncon-cerned. "Are you one of those concertinas?"

"I'm a concierge," Klaus said, not bothering to explain that a concertina is a kind of accordion. "Can I be of assistance?"

"Of course you can be of assistance!" the voice called back. "That's why I rang for you! Enter at once!"

Klaus, of course, did not want to enter a room that was filled with smoke, but working, even for the purposes of secretly observing the mysteries of a hotel, usually means doing things you do not want to do, so the middle Baudelaire opened the door, releasing an enormous amount of smoke into the hallway, and took a few hesitant steps into the room. Through the smoke he could see a short figure, dressed in a suit of shiny green cloth, standing at the far end of the room, facing the window. Behind his back he held a cigar that was clearly responsible for all the smoke wafting past Klaus into the hallway. But Klaus did not care about the smoke. He hardly even noticed it. He merely stared in dismay at the person standing at the window, a person he had hoped he would never see again.

You have probably heard the tiresome expression "It's a small world," which people use to explain a coincidence. For instance, if you walk into an Italian restaurant and encounter a waiter you recognize, the waiter might cry, "It's a small world!" as if it were unavoidable that the two of you would be at the same restaurant at the same time. But if you've ever taken even the shortest of walks, you know the truth of the matter. It is not a small world. It is a large world, and there are Italian restaurants sprinkled all over it, employing waiters who have crucial messages for you and waiters who are trying to make sure you never receive them, and these pairs of waiters are engaged in an argument that began many years ago, when you were so young that it was not safe to feed you even the softest of gnocchi. The world is not small but enormous, and Klaus had hoped that this enormous world was big enough that a guest of the Hotel

Denouement employed in the lumber industry and staying in Room 674 would not be the horrid man who had employed him and his sisters at Lucky Smells Lumbermill. During their dreadful stay in Paltryville, the Baudelaires never saw the man's face, which was always covered by a cloud of smoke from his cigar, and they never learned the man's real name, which was so difficult to pronounce that he made everyone call him "Sir," but they learned plenty about his greedy and cruel behavior, and Klaus was not happy to learn that this enormous world was going to treat him to another helping of Sir's selfishness.

"Well, don't just stand there!" Sir shouted. "Ask what you can do for me!"

"What can I do for you, Sir?" Klaus asked.

Sir whirled around, and the cloud around his head whirled around, too. "How did you know my name?" he asked suspiciously.

"The concierge didn't know your name," said another voice patiently, and Klaus saw, through the smoke, a second person he had not noticed, sitting on the bed in a bathrobe with HOTEL DENOUEMENT embroidered on the back. This man was also familiar from the Baudelaires' days at Lucky Smells, although Klaus did not know whether to be happy to see him or not. On one hand, Charles had always been kind to the children, and although his kindness had not been enough to save them from danger, it is always a relief to discover there is a kind person in the room that you had not noticed previously. On the other hand, however, Klaus was sorry to see that Charles was still partners with Sir, who enjoyed bossing around Charles almost as much as he did the Baudelaires. "I'm sure the concierge calls all the male guests in this hotel 'sir.'"

"Of course he does!" Sir shouted. "I'm not an idiot! Now then, concertina, we want to be taken to the sauna right away!"

"Yes sir," Klaus said, grateful that either Frank or Ernest had mentioned that the sauna was in Room 613. A sauna is a room constructed out of wood and kept very, very hot, in which people can sit in steam, which is believed to be beneficial to one's health, and Klaus would have found it very difficult to find such a room in the Hotel Denouement without a catalog. "The sauna should be down the hall, on the opposite side," Klaus said. "If you gentlemen will follow me, I'll take you there."

"I'm sorry we made you come all the way to our rooms just to take us right down the hall," Charles said.

"It's my pleasure," Klaus said. As I'm sure you know, when people say, "It's my pleasure," they usually mean something along the lines of, "There's nothing on Earth I would rather do less," but the middle Baudelaire was hoping that he could learn why the Baudelaires' former guardian and his partner had journeyed from Paltryville to the Hotel Denouement.

"Let's go this very instant!" Sir shouted, marching out into the hallway.

"Don't you want to change into a bathing

suit?" Charles asked. "If you're fully clothed, you won't get the health benefits of the steam."

"I don't care about the health benefits of the steam!" Sir shouted. "I'm not an idiot! I just love the smell of hot wood!"

Charles sighed, and followed Klaus out of Room 674 and into the hallway. "I was hoping my partner would relax during our stay here," he said, "but I'm afraid he's taking a busman's holiday."

"Busman's holiday" is an expression which refers to when people do the same thing on vacation that they do in their everyday lives, such as plumbers who visit the Museum of Sinks, or villains who disguise themselves even on their days off. But Klaus could not believe that these two men were merely vacationing in the Hotel Denouement, just two days before V.F.D. was to gather. "Are you here on business?" he asked, hoping that Charles would keep talking as they approached the sauna.

"Don't tell that concertina anything!" Sir

cried, continuing to use the word for "accordion" instead of the word for "hotel employee." "He's supposed to be at our beck and call, not nosing around in our business like a spy!"

"Forgive me, Sir," Klaus said, as calmly as he could. "We've arrived at the sauna."

Sure enough, Klaus, Sir, and Charles had arrived at Room 613, which had a mass of steam pouring out of the gap between the door and the floor, like a mirror image of Sir's cigar smoke pouring out of Room 674. "You can wait outside, concertina," said Sir. "We'll shout for you when we're ready to be escorted back to our room."

"We don't need to be escorted," Charles said timidly, opening the door. Inside, Klaus could see nothing but a mass of whirling steam. "It's just down the hallway. I'm sure the concierge has enough to do without waiting around for us."

"But someone has to hold my cigar!" Sir shouted. "I can't walk into a room full of steam with a head full of smoke! I'm not an idiot!"

"Of course not," Charles said with a sigh,

and walked into the sauna. Sir handed Klaus the cigar and strode into the sauna before the cloud of smoke around his head could clear. Behind him, the door started to close, but Klaus thought quickly and stuck out his foot. The door remained open just a crack, and as quietly as he could he swung the door back open and slipped inside, pausing to balance Sir's cigar on the rim of one of the ornamental vases. As he suspected, the steam was so thick inside the sauna that he could not see Sir or his partner, which meant the Paltryville citizens could not see him, either, while they sat and talked in the heated room. It was a flaneur's perfect opportunity to eavesdrop on a private conversation.

"I wish you could be more polite," Charles said, his voice drifting through the steam. "There was no reason to accuse that concierge of being a spy."

"I was just trying to be cautious!" Sir said gruffly, a word which here means "in a tone that indicated he had no intention of being more polite." Klaus heard the crinkle of his shiny suit, and imagined that the lumbermill owner was shrugging. "You're the one who said enemies might be lurking in this hotel!"

"That's what I was told in the letter I received," Charles said. "According to J. S., we must be very cautious if we want to find the Baudelaires."

Klaus was grateful that his amazed expression was hidden in the steam. The middle Baudelaire could not imagine why the mysterious impostor J. S. was helping Charles find him and his sisters, and if it had not been so hot in the sauna he would have broken out in a cold sweat, a phrase which here means "felt very nervous about the conversation he was observing."

"I don't want to find the Baudelaires!" Sir said. "Those orphans were nothing but trouble for the lumbermill!"

"They weren't the cause of the trouble," Charles said. "Count Olaf was. Don't you remember?"

"Of course I remember!" Sir cried. "I'm not an idiot! Count Olaf disguised himself as a rather attractive young lady, and worked with that sinister hypnotist to cause accidents in my mill! If the Baudelaires didn't have that fortune waiting for them in the bank, Olaf never would have done all that mischief! It's the orphans' fault!"

"I suppose you're right," Charles said, "but I still would like to find them. According to *The Daily Punctilio*, the Baudelaires are in a heap of trouble."

"According to *The Daily Punctilio*," Sir said, "the Baudelaires are murderers! For all we know, that bookworm with the eyeglasses could sneak up on us right here in the hotel and kill us to death!"

"The children aren't going to murder us," Charles said, "although after their experiences at Lucky Smells I could hardly blame them. In fact, if I manage to find them, the first thing I'll do is give them my sincere apologies. Perhaps I can ask one of the concierges for a pair of binoculars. J. S. said they might be arriving by submarine, so I could watch for a periscope rising from the sea."

"I wish our room had a view of the pond instead," Sir said. "When I'm done with a cigar, I like to drop the butt into a calm body of water and watch the pretty ripples."

"I'm not sure that would be good for the pond," Charles said.

"What do I care about the pond?" Sir demanded. "I have better things to do than worry about the environment. The Finite Forest is running low on trees, so business is bad for the lumbermill. The last big order we had was for building that horseradish factory, and that was a very long time ago. I'm hoping Thursday's cocktail party will be an excellent opportunity to do some business. After all, if it weren't for my lumber, this hotel wouldn't even exist!"

"I remember," Charles said. "We had to deliver the lumber in the middle of the night.

But Sir, you told me you never heard from that organization again."

"I didn't," Sir said, "until now. You're not the only one who gets notes from this fellow J. S. I'm invited to a party he's hosting on Thursday night, and he said I should bring all my valuables. That must mean plenty of rich people will be there—rich people who might want to buy some lumber."

"Perhaps if the lumbermill becomes more successful," Charles said, "we could pay our employees with money, instead of just gum and coupons."

"Don't be an idiot!" Sir said. "Gum and coupons is a fair deal! If you spent less time reading and more time thinking about lumber, you'd care more about money and less about people!"

"There's nothing wrong with caring about people," Charles said quietly. "I care about you, Sir. And I care about the Baudelaires. If what J. S. wrote is true, then their parents—"

"Excuse me." The door of the sauna swung open, and Klaus saw a tall, dim figure step into the steam.

"Is that my concertina?" Sir barked. "I told you to wait outside!"

"No, I'm one of the managers of the hotel," said either Frank or Ernest. "We do have a concertina available in Room 786, if you're interested in musical instruments. I'm sorry to interrupt your afternoon, but I'm afraid I must ask all guests to vacate the sauna. A situation has arisen that requires the use of this room. If you are interested in steam, there's quite a bit of it in Room—"

"I don't care about steam!" cried Sir. "I just like smelling hot wood! Where else can I smell hot wood, except in the sauna?"

"Room 547 is dedicated to organic chemistry," replied the manager. "There are all sorts of smelly things there."

Klaus quickly opened the sauna door and pretended to walk inside. "I'd be happy to take our guests to Room 547," he said, hoping to observe the rest of Sir and Charles's conversation.

"No, no," the manager said. "You're needed here, concierge. By a strange coincidence there happens to be a chemist standing in the hallway who would be happy to escort these two gentlemen."

"Oh, all right!" Sir said, and stomped out of the sauna, where a figure stood in a long, white coat and a mask such as surgeons or chemists wear over their noses and mouths. Sir reached down and picked up his cigar from the ornamental vase, restoring the cloud of smoke to his face just as the cloud of steam evaporated, and without another word he and his partner followed the chemist away from the sauna, leaving Klaus alone with the volunteer or villain.

"Be very careful with this," said either Frank or Ernest, handing a large, rigid object to Klaus. It was something flat and wide, rolled into a thick tube like a sleeping bag. "When it's unrolled, the surface is very sticky—so sticky that anything it touches becomes trapped. Do you know what this is called?"

"Flypaper," Klaus said, remembering a book he had read about the adventures of an exterminator. "Is the hotel having an insect problem?"

"Our problem is not with insects," the manager said. "It's with birds. This is birdpaper. I need you to attach one end to the windowsill of this room, and dangle the rest outside, over the pond. Can you guess why?"

"To trap birds," Klaus said.

"You're obviously very well-read," said Ernest or Frank, although it was impossible to tell whether he was impressed or disgusted with this fact. "So you know that birds can cause all sorts of problems. For instance, I've heard about a swarm of eagles that recently stole a great crowd of children. What do you think of that?"

Klaus gasped. He knew, of course, exactly what he thought of the great swarm of eagles who kidnapped a troop of Snow Scouts while the Baudelaires were living on Mount Fraught. He thought it was horrid, but the face on the volunteer or villain was so unfathomable that the middle Baudelaire could not tell if the manager thought so, too. "I think it's remarkable," Klaus said finally, carefully choosing a word which here means either wonderful or horrible.

"That's a remarkable answer," replied either Frank or Ernest, and then Klaus heard the manager sigh thoughtfully. "Tell me," he said, "are you who I think you are?"

Klaus blinked behind his glasses, and behind the sunglasses that lay on top of them. Deciding on a safe answer to a question is like deciding on a safe ingredient in a sandwich, because if you make the wrong decision you may find that something horrible is coming out of your mouth. As Klaus stood in the sauna, he wanted nothing more than to decide on a safe answer, such as "Yes, I'm Klaus Baudelaire," if he were talking to Frank, or "I'm sorry I don't know what you're talking about," if he were talking to Ernest. But he knew there was no way to tell if either of those answers was safe, so he opened his mouth and uttered the only other answer he could think of.

"Of course I'm who you think I am," he said, feeling as if he were talking in code, although in a code he did not know. "I'm a concierge."

"I see," said Frank or Ernest, as unfathomable as ever. "I'm grateful for your assistance, concierge. Not many people have the courage to help with a scheme like this."

Without another word, the manager left, and Klaus was alone in the sauna. Carefully, he walked through the steam and felt his way to the window, which he managed to unlatch and open, swinging a shutter marked ∂ out over the pond. As will happen when a very hot room is exposed to cold air, the steam raced through the window and evaporated. With the steam gone, Klaus could see the wooden walls and benches that comprised the sauna, and he only wished that everything were as clear in his own head as it was in Room 613. In silence, he attached one end of the birdpaper to the windowsill, his head spinning with his mysterious observations as a flaneur and his mysterious errand as a concierge, and in silence he dangled the rest outside, where it curved stiffly over the pond like a slide at a playground. In silence he gazed at this strange arrangement, and wondered which manager had requested such an odd task. But before he could leave the sauna, Klaus's silence was shattered by an enormous noise.

The clock in the lobby of the Hotel Denouement is the stuff of legend, a phrase which here means "very famous for being very loud." It is located in the very center of the ceiling, at the very top of the dome, and when the clock announces the hour, its bells clang throughout the entire building, making an immense, deep noise that sounds like a certain word being uttered once for each hour. At this particular moment, it was three o'clock, and everyone in the hotel could hear the booming ring of the enormous bells of the clock, uttering the word three times in succession: *Wrong! Wrong! Wrong!*

As he turned away from the sauna's open window and walked back down the hall toward the elevator doors, Klaus Baudelaire felt as if the clock were scolding him for his efforts at solving the mysteries of the Hotel Denouement. *Wrong!* He had tried his best to be a flaneur, but hadn't observed enough to know exactly what Sir and Charles were doing at the hotel. *Wrong!* He had tried to communicate with one of the hotel's managers, but had been unable to discover whether he was Frank or Ernest. And—most *Wrong!* of all—he had performed his errand as a concierge, and now a strip of birdpaper was dangling out of the Hotel Denouement, where it would serve some unknown, sinister purpose. With each strike of the clock, Klaus felt wronger and wronger, and as he stepped inside the small elevator, he frowned in thought. He dearly hoped his two siblings had found more success in their errands, for as he walked through the sliding doors and pressed the button to return to the lobby, all the middle Baudelaire could think was that everything was wrong, wrong, wrong.

CHAPTER
Six

When the elevator reached the third story, Sunny bid good-bye to her siblings and stepped out into a long, empty hallway. Numbered doors lined the hallway, odd numbers on one side and even numbers on the other, as well as large, ornamental vases that were taller than Sunny but not nearly as charming. The youngest Baudelaire walked on the smooth, gray carpet in nervous, uncertain steps. Pretending to be a concierge in order to be a flaneur, in the hopes of unraveling a mystery unfolding in an enormous, perplexing hotel, was a difficult enough task for her older siblings, but it was particularly difficult for someone just growing out of baby-hood. Over the past few months, Sunny Baude-laire had improved her walking abilities, adopted a more standard vocabulary, and even learned how to cook, but she was still unsure whether she could successfully pass for a hotel profes-sional. As she approached the guests who had rung for a concierge, she decided that she would adopt a taciturn demeanor, a phrase which here means "only communicate when absolutely nec-essary, so as not to call attention to her youth and relative inexperience in employment."

When Sunny reached Room 371 she thought at first there had been some mistake. Down in the lobby, either Frank or Ernest had told the Baudelaires that educational guests were stay-ing in that particular room, but the youngest Baudelaire could not imagine what educational purpose could explain the unearthly sounds coming from behind the door, unless perhaps a teacher was giving a class on how to torture a small animal. Someone—or something—in

Room 371 was making dreadful squeaks, strange moans, piercing whistles, irritating shrieks, mysterious mutterings, and, suddenly, a melodic hum or two, and the sounds were so loud that it was a moment before anyone heard Sunny's gloved fists knocking on the door.

"Who dares interrupt a genius when he's rehearsing?" said a voice that was loud, booming, and strangely familiar.

"Concierge," Sunny called.

"*Concierge*," the voice mimicked back to Sunny, in a high, squealing tone that the Baudelaire recognized instantly, and to her dismay the door opened and there stood a person she had hoped she would never encounter again.

If you have ever worked someplace and then, later, not worked there, then you know there are three ways you can leave a job: you can quit, you can be fired, or you can exit by mutual agreement. "Quit," as I'm sure you know, is a word which means that you were disappointed with your employer. "Fired," of course, is a

word which means that your employer was disappointed with you. And "exit by mutual agreement" is a phrase which means that you wanted
to quit, and your employer wanted to fire you,
and that you ran out of the office, factory, or
monastery before anyone could decide who got
to go first. In any case, no matter which method
you use to leave a job, it is never pleasant to run
into a former employer, because it reminds both
of you of all the miserable time you spent working together. I once threw myself down a flight
of stairs rather than face even one moment with
a milliner, at whose shop I quit working after
discovering the sinister truth about her berets,
only to find that the paramedic who repaired
my fractured arm was a man who had fired me
from a job playing accordion in his orchestra
after only two and half performances of a certain opera. It would be difficult to say whether
Sunny ended her brief stint—a word which
here means "dreadful period of time"—working as an administrative assistant at Prufrock

Preparatory School by quitting, getting fired, or exiting by mutual agreement, as she and her siblings were removed from the boarding school after a scheme of Count Olaf's almost succeeded, but it was still unpleasant to be face-to-face with Vice Principal Nero after all this time.

"What do you want?" Nero demanded, brandishing the violin that had been making all that dreadful noise. Sunny was not pleased to see that Nero's four pigtails, which were quite short when she had first made the vice principal's acquaintance, had grown into long, stringy braids, and that he still liked to wear a necktie decorated with pictures of snails.

"You rang," Sunny said, as taciturnly as she could.

"*You rang,*" Nero mimicked immediately. "Well, so what if I did? Ringing for you is no excuse for interrupting me while I'm practicing the violin. I have a very important violin recital on Thursday, and I plan on rehearsing every moment until then."

"Please, boss," said another familiar voice, and Nero turned around, his greasy braids swinging behind him. Sunny saw, to her dismay, that Nero was sharing Room 371 with two other figures from the Baudelaires' past. "You said we could stop for a lunch break," continued Mr. Remora, who had been Violet's teacher at Prufrock Preparatory School, although it would be difficult to say exactly what kind of teacher he was, as all he liked to do was tell short, pointless stories, and eat banana after banana, occasionally smearing the yellow pulp all over his mustache, which was as dark and thick as a gorilla's thumb.

"I'm so hungry I could eat a dekagram of rice," said Mrs. Bass, who had been Klaus's teacher. It was clear that her enthusiasm for measuring things according to the metric system had remained the same, but the youngest Baudelaire noticed that her appearance had changed somewhat. On top of her shaggy, black hair was a small blond wig, like a snowcap on the top of a mountain peak, and she was wearing a small, narrow mask with two tiny holes for her eyes. "I've heard there's a wonderful Indian restaurant in Room 954."

Normally, Sunny would have replied with "Andiamo," which was her way of saying, "I'd be happy to take you there," but she was afraid that her manner of speaking would give away her true identity, so instead she continued her taciturn demeanor by giving the three guests a little bow, and gesturing down the hallway with one of her gloves. Vice Principal Nero looked disappointed, but then gave Sunny a simpering glance and mimicked her gestures in an insulting way, proving he could mock someone even if they didn't speak.

"Don't you think you should bring your loot, Mrs. Bass?" asked Mr. Remora, pointing to the far wall of Room 371.

"No, no," Mrs. Bass said quickly, her eyes blinking nervously through the holes in the mask. "It'll be safer in the room."

Sunny tilted her head so she could stare past the teacher's knees, and made her first important observation as a flaneur. Piled on a table in the hotel room, right near a window overlooking the sea, was a large, bulky pile of large, bulky bags, each with the words PROPERTY OF MULCTUARY MONEY MANAGEMENT stamped on them in stern black ink. The youngest Baudelaire could not imagine why Mrs. Bass was in possession of something from the bank where Mr. Poe worked, but with two teachers and one vice principal waiting impatiently in the hallway, she had no time to stop and think. With another taciturn gesture, she quickly led the guests toward the elevator, grateful that Mrs. Bass knew the location of the restaurant. The youngest Baudelaire would have had no idea how to find an Indian restaurant in the Hotel Denouement without a catalog.

"I'm very excited about my recital," Vice Principal Nero said, as the small elevator began its journey to the ninth story. "I'm sure all of the music critics at the cocktail party will love my performance. As soon as I'm recognized as a genius, I can finally quit my job at Prufrock Prep!"

"How do you know there will be music critics at the party?" Mr. Remora asked. "My invitation just said there'd be an all-you-can-eat banana buffet."

"Mine didn't say anything about music critics, either," Mrs. Bass said. "It just says that there's a party in celebration of the metric system, and that I should bring as many valuables as possible so they could be measured. As a teacher, I don't earn enough money to purchase any valuables, so I had to resort to a life of crime."

"*I had to resort to a life of crime*," Nero mimicked. "I can't believe a genius like myself was invited to the same party as you two. Esmé Squalor and her boyfriend must have accidentally mailed you those invitations."

Sunny's eyes narrowed in thought behind her enormous sunglasses. Esmé Squalor's boyfriend, of course, was none other than Count Olaf. After so much time struggling against his villainous schemes, the youngest Baudelaire was not surprised to hear that Olaf was planning further treachery, but she could not imagine why he was luring her former employer to the hotel. She would have loved to continue her observations as a flaneur, but as the elevator came to a stop, she had to return to her duties as a concierge, and utter at least one taciturn word.

"Nine," she said.

"*Nine*," Nero mimicked, and pushed his way to the front so he could exit the elevator first. Sunny followed, and quickly guided the three guests to the door numbered 954, which she opened with a silent flourish.

"Can I help you?" asked a wavering voice, and Sunny was astonished to recognize yet another person from the Baudelaires' past. He was a very old man, wearing very tiny glasses, each lens scarcely larger than a green pea. When the children had first met this man, he had not been wearing a hat of any kind, but today he had wrapped a length of cloth around his head and secured it in place with a shiny red jewel. Sunny remembered such a turban on the head of Count Olaf when he had disguised himself as a gym teacher, but she could not guess why such a thing would be worn by the man the Baudelaires had met at Heimlich Hospital.

"*Can I help you?*" Nero mimicked. "Of course you can help us! We're starving!"

"I didn't realize this was a sad occasion," said Hal, squinting through his glasses.

"It won't be a sad occasion if you feed us," Mr. Remora said.

Hal frowned, as if Mr. Remora had given the wrong response, but he quickly ushered the three guests to a wooden table in the otherwise deserted restaurant. "We are proud to serve a wide variety of Indian dishes," he said, handing out menus and pouring everyone a glass of water. "The culinary history of the region is quite interesting, actually. When the British—"

"I'll have ten grams of rice," Mrs. Bass interrupted, "one tenth of a hectogram of shrimp vindaloo, a dekagram of chana aloo masala, one thousand centigrams of tandoori salmon, four samosas with a surface area of ninteen cubic centimeters, five deciliters of mango lassi, and a sada rava dosai that's exactly nineteen centimeters long."

Sunny hoped Hal would talk about some of the dishes Mrs. Bass had ordered, so her observations as a flaneur might also improve her cooking skills, but he merely wrote down her order without comment and turned to Mr. Remora, who was frowning at the menu.

"I'll have forty-eight orders of fried bananas," he said, after much thought.

"Interesting choice," Hal commented. "And you, sir?"

"A bag of candy!" Vice Principal Nero demanded. Sunny had almost forgotten that her former employer enjoyed demanding candy from anyone he could.

"Candy is not a traditional Indian dish," Hal said. "If you're not sure what to order, allow me to recommend the combination plate."

"*Allow me to recommend the combination plate!*" Nero mimicked, glaring at Hal. "Never mind. I won't eat anything! It's probably dangerous to eat candy from foreigners!"

Hal did not reply to this bout of xeno-phobia—a word for a fear or disgust of foreign cultures that Jerome Squalor had taught the Baudelaires a while ago—but merely nodded. "Your lunches will be ready shortly," he said. "I'll be in the kitchen if you need anything."

"*I'll be in the kitchen if you need anything,*" Nero mimicked immediately, as Hal walked through a pair of swinging doors. With a sigh, he moved his water glass off his placemat and onto the wooden table, where it was sure to leave a ring, and turned to the two teachers. "That foreigner's head reminds me of that nice man Coach Genghis."

"Nice man?" Mr. Remora asked. "If I remember correctly, he was a notorious villain in disguise."

Mrs. Bass reached up and nervously adjusted her wig. "Just because someone is a criminal," she said, "does not mean they're not a nice person. Besides, if you're on the run from the law, you're bound to get cranky from time to time."

"Speaking of running from the law—" Mr. Remora said, but the vice principal cut off his sentence with a glare.

"We'll talk about that later," he said quickly, and then turned to Sunny. "Concierge, go get us some napkins," he said, clearly inventing an excuse to get the youngest Baudelaire out of earshot. "Just because I'm not eating doesn't mean I can't get food on my chin!"

Sunny nodded taciturnly, and walked toward the swinging doors. As a flaneur, she was sorry to halt her observations, particularly when the guests of Room 371 seemed about to discuss something important. But as a budding gourmand—a phrase which here means "young girl with a strong interest in cooking"—she was eager to get a look at a restaurant kitchen. Ever since Justice Strauss had taken the Baudelaires to the market in order to buy ingredients to make puttanesca sauce, Sunny had been interested in the culinary arts, although it was only recently that she had matured enough to develop this interest. If you have never taken a peek inside a restaurant kitchen, it is something you may want to try, because it is full of interesting items and it is usually quite easy to sneak in, providing that you don't mind being glared at if you are discovered. But when Sunny stepped through the swinging doors, she did not notice a single interesting item in the kitchen. For one thing, the kitchen was swirling with steam, from a dozen pots that were boiling in every corner of the room. The cloudy air made it difficult to see much of anything, but that was not the main reason Sunny was ignoring the culinary equipment. There was a conversation going on between two unfathomable figures in the room, and what was being said was far more interesting than any ingredient or gadget used in preparing traditional Indian dishes.

"I have news from J. S.," either Frank or Ernest was whispering to Hal. Both men were standing with their backs to Sunny and leaning in toward one another so they could talk as quietly as possible. Sunny maneuvered into the middle of a particularly thick cloud of steam so that she wouldn't be seen.

"J. S.?" Hal said. "She's here?"

"She's here to help," the manager corrected. "She's been using her Vision Furthering Device to watch the skies, and I'm afraid she reports that we will all be eating crow."

"I'm sorry to hear that," Hal said. "Crow is a tough bird to cook, because the meat is very muscular from all the carrying that crows do."

Sunny scratched her head with one glove in puzzlement. The expression "eating crow" simply means "enduring humiliation," and the youngest Baudelaire had learned it from her parents, who liked to tease each other after playing one another at backgammon. "Bertrand," Sunny could remember her mother saying, tossing the dice to the ground in triumph, "I have won again. Prepare to eat crow." Then, with a gleam in her eyes, she would pounce on Sunny's father and tickle him, while the Baudelaire children piled on top of their parents in a laughing heap. But Hal seemed to be discussing the eating of crow as an actual culinary dish, rather than a figure of speech, and the youngest Baudelaire wondered if there were more to this Indian restaurant than she had thought.

"It is a shame," agreed either Frank or Ernest. "If only there was something that could make the dish a little sweeter. I've heard that certain mushrooms are available."

"Sugar would be better than mushrooms," Hal said unfathomably.

"According to our calculations, the sugar will be laundered sometime after nightfall," replied the manager, equally unfathomably.

"I'm glad," Hal said. "My job's been difficult enough. Do you know how many leaves of lettuce I've had to send up to the roof?"

Frank or Ernest frowned. "Tell me," he said, in an even more quiet tone of voice. "Are you who I think you are?"

"Are *you* who *I* think you are?" replied Hal, equally quietly.

Sunny crept closer, hoping to hear more of the conversation to learn if either Frank or Ernest was referring to the Medusoid Mycelium, which was a type of mushroom, or if Hal was referring to the sugar bowl. But to the youngest Baudelaire's dismay the floor creaked slightly, and the cloud of steam swirled away, and Hal and Ernest, or perhaps Frank, spun around to gasp at her.

"Are you who I think you are?" said the two men in unison.

One of the advantages of being taciturn is that it is rare for your words to get you into trouble. A taciturn writer, for instance, might produce only one short poem every ten years, which is unlikely to annoy anyone, whereas someone who writes twelve or thirteen books in a relatively short time is likely to find themselves hiding under the coffee table of a notorious villain, holding his breath, hoping nobody at the cocktail party will notice the trembling backgammon set, and wondering, as the ink-stain spreads across the carpeting, if certain literary exercises have been entirely worthwhile. If Sunny had decided to adopt a chatty demeanor, she would have had to think of a lengthy reply to the question she had just been asked, and she could not imagine what that reply might be. If she knew that the manager in the kitchen was Frank, she would say something along the lines of, "Sunny Baudelaire please help," which was her way of saying, "Yes, I'm Sunny Baudelaire, and my siblings and I need your help uncovering the mysterious plot unfolding in the Hotel Denouement, and signaling our findings to the members of V.F.D." If she knew that it was Ernest who was staring at her, she would say something more like, "No Habla Esperanto," which was her way of saying, "I'm sorry; I don't know what you're talking about." The presence of Hal, of course, made the situation even more complicated, because the children had exited their employment at Heimlich Hospital's Library of Records by mutual agreement, as Hal believed that they were responsible for lighting the Library of Records on fire, and the Baudelaires needed to flee the hospital as quickly as possible, but Sunny had no way of knowing if Hal continued to hold a grudge—a phrase which here means "was an enemy of the Baudelaires"—or if he was working at the hotel as a volunteer. But Sunny had adopted a taciturn demeanor, and a taciturn answer was all that was required.

"Concierge," she said, and that was enough. Hal looked at Frank, or perhaps it was Ernest, and Ernest, or perhaps it was Frank, looked back at Hal. The two men nodded, and then crossed to a shiny cabinet at the far end of the kitchen. Hal opened the cabinet and handed a large, strange object to either Frank or Ernest, who looked it over and handed it to Sunny. The object was like a large, metal spider, with curly wires spreading out in all directions, but where the head of the spider might have been was the keyboard of a typewriter.

"Do you know what this is?" asked the villain or volunteer.

"Yes," the youngest Baudelaire said. Sunny had never seen such a device, but her siblings had described the strange lock they had encountered in a secret passageway hidden deep within the Mortmain Mountains. Had it not been for Violet's knowledge of science and Klaus's remarkable memory for Russian literature, they might never have opened the lock, and Sunny would still be Count Olaf's captive.

"Be very careful with it," said either Frank or Ernest. "When you place this device on the knob of an ordinary door, and press the letters V, F, and D, it will become a Vernacularly Fastened Door. I want you to take the elevator to the basement, and vernacularly fasten Room 025."

"That's the laundry room, you know," said Hal, squinting at Sunny through his glasses. "As with many laundry rooms, there's a vent, which funnels the steam from all the washing machines to the outside, so the room doesn't overheat."

"But if something were to fall from the sky at just the right angle," said Frank or Ernest, "it might fall down the funnel and into the room. And if that something were very valuable, then the room ought to be locked up tight, so that the item would not fall into the wrong hands."

Sunny Baudelaire had no idea what these two adults were talking about, and wished that she were still standing unnoticed in the steam, so she could observe the rest of their conversation. But she gripped the strange lock in her gloved hands and knew that it was not time to be a flaneur.

"I'm grateful for your assistance, concierge," Frank said, or maybe it was Ernest, or maybe the man answering was neither brother. "Not many people have the courage to help with a scheme like this."

Sunny gave one more taciturn nod, and turned to exit the kitchen. In silence she walked through the swinging doors and across the restaurant, not even pausing to listen to the whispered conversation Vice Principal Nero was having with Mr. Remora and Mrs. Bass, and in silence she opened the door to Room 954 and walked down the hallway to the elevator. It was only when she was traveling down to the basement that Sunny's silence was shattered by an enormous noise.

The clock in the lobby of the Hotel Denouement is the stuff of legend, a phrase which here means "very famous for being very loud." It is located in the very center of the ceiling, at the very top of the dome, and when the clock announces the hour, its bells clang throughout the entire building, making an immense, deep noise that sounds like a certain word being uttered once for each hour. At this particular moment, it was three o'clock, and everyone in the hotel could hear the booming ring of the enormous bells of the clock, uttering the word three times in succession: *Wrong! Wrong! Wrong!*

As she walked through the sliding doors of the elevator and down the basement hallway, past the ornamental vases and numbered doors, Sunny Baudelaire felt as if the clock were scolding her for her efforts at solving the mysteries of the Hotel Denouement. *Wrong!* She had tried her best to be a flaneur, but hadn't observed enough to discover what two teachers and a vice principal from Prufrock Preparatory School were doing at the hotel. *Wrong!* She had tried to communicate with one of the hotel's managers, but had been unable to discover whether he was Frank or Ernest, or whether Hal was a volunteer or an enemy. And—most *Wrong!* of all—she was performing an errand as a concierge, and was now turning the entrance to the laundry room into a Vernacularly Fastened Door for some unknown, sinister purpose. With each strike of the clock, Sunny felt wronger and wronger, until at last she reached Room 025, where a washerwoman with long, blond hair and rumpled clothing was just shutting the door on her way out. With a hurried nod, the washerwoman padded down the hallway. Sunny dearly hoped her two siblings had found more success in their errands, for as she placed the lock on the doorknob, and typed the letters V-F-D into the typewriter keyboard, all the youngest Baudelaire could think was that everything was wrong, wrong, wrong.

At this point, the history of the Baudelaire orphans reverts to its sequential format, and if you are interested in finishing the story, you should read the chapters in the order in which they appear, although I dearly hope you are not interested in finishing the story, any more than the story is interested in finishing you.

CHAPTER Seven

Quite a few things happened that day after the clock struck three and each *Wrong!* echoed throughout the immense and perplexing world of the Hotel Denouement. On the ninth story, a woman was suddenly recognized by a chemist, and the two of them had a fit of giggles. In the base-ment, a strange sight was reported by an ambidextrous man who spoke into a walkie-talkie. On the sixth story, one of the

housekeepers removed a disguise, and drilled a hole behind an ornamental vase in order to examine the cables that held one of the elevators in place, while listening to the faint sound of a very annoying song coming from a room just above her. In Room 296, a volunteer suddenly realized that the Hebrew language is read from right to left rather than left to right, which meant that it should be read from left to right rather than right to left in the mirror, and in the coffee shop, located in Room 178, a villain requested sugar in his coffee, was immediately thrown to the floor so a waitress could see if he had a tattoo on his ankle, and then received an apology and a free slice of rhubarb pie for all his trouble. In Room 174, a banker picked up the phone only to find no one on the line, and in Room 594, a family sat unnoticed among tanks of tropical fish, with only a suitcase of dirty laundry for company, unaware that underneath a cushion of a sofa in the lobby was the doily for which they had been searching for more than nine years. Just outside the hotel, a taxi driver gazed down at the funnel spouting steam into the sky, and wondered if a certain man with an unusually shaped back would ever return and claim the suitcases that still lay in the trunk, and on the other side of the hotel, a woman in a diving helmet and a shiny suit shone a flashlight through the water and tried to see to the murky bottom of the sea. At the opposite end of the city, a long, black automobile took a woman away from a man she loved, and in another city, miles and miles from the Baudelaires, four children played at the beach, unaware that they were about to receive some very dreadful news, and in yet another city, neither the one where the Baudelaires lived nor the one I just mentioned, someone else learned something and there was some sort of fuss, or so I have been led to believe. With each *Wrong!* of the clock, as the afternoon slipped into evening, countless things happened, not only in the immense and perplexing world of the

Hotel Denouement, but also in the immense and perplexing world that lay outside its brick walls, but the Baudelaire orphans did not think of any of these things. Curiously, their errands as concierges kept them in the lobby for the rest of the afternoon, so they had no more occasion to venture into the small elevators and observe anything further as flaneurs, and spent the hours fetching things back and forth across the lobby, but the siblings did not think of the objects they were fetching, or the guests who were waiting for them, or even the tall, skinny figure of either Frank or Ernest, who would occasionally rush by them on errands of his own. As evening approached, and the bells behind their desk rang less and less frequently, Violet, Klaus, and Sunny thought only of the things that had happened to them. They thought only of what each of them had observed, and they wondered what in the world it all might mean.

Finally, just as either Frank or Ernest had predicted, night arrived and the hotel grew very quiet, and the three siblings gathered behind the large, wooden desk to talk, leaning their backs against the wall and stretching out their legs until their feet almost touched the bells. Violet told the story of Esmé Squalor, Carmelita Spats, and Geraldine Julienne in the rooftop sunbathing salon, and either Frank or Ernest in the lobby. Klaus told the story of Sir and Charles in Room 674, and either Frank or Ernest in the sauna. And Sunny told the story of Vice Principal Nero, Mr. Remora, and Mrs. Bass in Room 371, and either Frank or Ernest, and Hal in the Indian restaurant in Room 954. Klaus took careful note of everything in his commonplace book, giving the book to Violet when it was his turn to speak, and all three Baudelaires interrupted each other with questions and ideas, but when all the stories had been told, and the children looked at the countless details inked onto the paper, everything that happened to them was as mysterious as it had been that morning.

"It just doesn't make any sense," Violet said. "Why is Esmé Squalor planning a party? Why did Carmelita Spats request a harpoon gun?"

"Why are Sir and Charles here?" Klaus asked. "Why is there birdpaper hanging out of the window of the sauna?"

"Why Nero?" Sunny asked. "Why Remora? Why Bass? Why Hal?"

"Who is J. S.?" Violet asked. "Is he a man lurking in the basement, or is she a woman watching the skies?"

"Where is Count Olaf?" Klaus asked. "Why has he invited so many of our former guardians here to the hotel?"

"Frankernest," Sunny said, and this was perhaps the most mysterious question of all. Violet, Klaus, and Sunny had each encountered one of the managers just moments before the clock struck three. Kit Snicket had told them that if they observed everyone they saw, they could tell the villains from the volunteers, but the Baudelaires did not know which sibling had encountered which manager, and they simply could not imagine how two people could be in three places at once. The Baudelaires pondered their situation in a silence broken only by a strange, repetitive sound that seemed to be coming from outside. For a moment, this sound was yet another mystery, but the siblings soon realized it was the croaking of frogs. The pond must have had thousands of frogs living in its depths, and now that night had arrived, the frogs had come to the surface and were communicating with one another in the guttural sound of their species. It was an unfathomable sound, as if even the natural world were a code the Baudelaires could not decipher.

"Kit said that all would not go well," Violet said. "She said our errands may be noble, but that we would not succeed."

"That's true," agreed Klaus. "She said all our hopes would go up in smoke, and maybe she was right. We each observed a different story, but none of the stories makes any sense."

"Elephant," Sunny said.

Violet and Klaus looked at their sister curiously.

"Poem," she said. "Father."

Violet and Klaus looked at one another in puzzlement.

"Elephant," Sunny insisted, but this was one of the rare occasions that Violet and Klaus did not understand what their sister was saying. The brow furrowed on Sunny's little forehead as she struggled to remember something that might help make herself clear to her siblings. Finally, she looked up at Violet and Klaus. "John Godfrey Saxe," she said, and all three Baudelaires smiled.

The name John Godfrey Saxe is not likely to mean anything to you, unless you are a fan of American humorist poets of the nineteenth century. There are not many such people in the world, but the Baudelaires' father was one of them, and had several poems committed to memory. From time to time he would get into a whimsical mood—the word "whimsical," as you probably know, means "odd and impulsive"—and would grab the nearest Baudelaire child, bounce him or her up and down on his lap, and recite a poem by John Godfrey Saxe about an elephant. In the poem, six blind men encountered an elephant for the first time and were unable to agree on what the animal was like. The first man felt the tall, smooth side of the elephant, and concluded that an elephant was like a wall. The second man felt the tusk of the elephant, and decided that an elephant resembled a spear. The third man felt the trunk of the elephant, and the fourth felt one of the elephant's legs, and so on and so on, with all of the blind men bickering over what an elephant is like. As with many children, Violet and Klaus had grown old enough to find their father's whimsical moods a little embarrassing, so Sunny had become the primary audience for Mr. Baudelaire's poetry recital, and remembered the poem best.

"That poem could have been written about us," Violet said. "We've each observed one tiny part of the puzzle, but none of us has seen the entire thing."

"Nobody could see the entire thing," Klaus said. "There's a mystery behind every door at the Hotel Denouement, and nobody can be everywhere at once, observing all the volunteers and all the villains."

"We've still got to try," Violet said. "Kit said that the sugar bowl was on its way to this hotel. We have to stop it from falling into the hands of the impostor."

"But the sugar bowl could be hidden any-where," Klaus said, "and the impostor could be anyone. Everyone we observed was talking about J. S., but we still don't know who he or she is."

"'Each was partly in the right,'" Sunny recited, from the penultimate verse of the ele-phant poem.

Her siblings smiled, and chimed in to finish the line. "'And all were in the wrong,'" they said together, but the last word was drowned out by another sound, or perhaps it would be more proper to say that the last "wrong" was drowned out by another. *Wrong!* called the clock of the Hotel Denouement. *Wrong! Wrong! Wrong! Wrong! Wrong! Wrong! Wrong! Wrong! Wrong! Wrong! Wrong!*

"It's late," Klaus said, as the twelfth *Wrong!* faded. "I hadn't realized we'd been talking for so long." He and his sisters stood up and stretched, and saw that the lobby had grown empty and silent. The lid of the grand piano was closed. The cascading fountain had been turned off. Even the reception desk was empty, as if the Hotel Denouement was not expecting any more guests until the morning. The light from the frog-shaped lamp, and of course the Baudelaires themselves, were the only signs of life underneath the enormous domed ceiling.

"I guess the guests are asleep," Violet said, "or they're staying up all night reading, like Frank said."

"Or Ernest," Sunny reminded her.

"Maybe we should try to sleep as well," Klaus said. "We have one more day to solve these mysteries, and we should be well-rested when that day arrives."

"I suppose there won't be much to observe after dark," Violet said.

"Tired," Sunny yawned.

The siblings nodded, but all three orphans just stood there. It did not seem right to sleep when so many enemies were lurking around the hotel, hatching sinister plots. But such events go on every night, not just in the Hotel Denouement but all over the world, and even the noblest of volunteers needs to get a little shut-eye, a phrase which here means "lie down behind a large, wooden desk and hope that nobody rings for the concierge until morning." The children would have preferred more comfortable sleeping circumstances, of course, but it had been a very long time since such circumstances were available, and so without any further discussion they bid one another good night, and Klaus reached up and turned off the frog-shaped lamp. For a moment the three children lay there in the darkness, listening to the croaking coming from the pond outside.

"It's dark," Sunny said. The youngest Baudelaire was not particularly afraid of the dark, but just felt like mentioning it, in case her siblings were nervous.

"It *is* dark," Violet agreed, with a yawn. "With my sunglasses on, it's as dark as—what did Kit Snicket say?—as dark as a crow flying through a pitch black night."

"That's it," Klaus said suddenly. His sisters heard him stand up in the dark, and then he turned the frog lamp back on, making them both blink behind their sunglasses.

"What's it?" Violet said. "I thought we were going to sleep."

"How can we sleep," Klaus asked, "when the sugar bowl is being delivered to the hotel this very night?"

"What?" Sunny asked. "How?"

Klaus pulled his commonplace book out of his pocket and flipped to the notes he had taken on what the Baudelaires had observed. "By crow," he said.

"Crow?" Violet said.

"It wouldn't be the first time crows have carried something important," Klaus said, reminding his sisters of the crows in the Village of Fowl Devotees, who had brought the Baudelaires messages from the Quagmires. "That's what Esmé Squalor has been watching for with her Vision Furthering Device."

"J. S. too," Sunny said, remembering what either Frank or Ernest had said about watching the skies.

"And that's why Carmelita Spats had me fetch a harpoon gun," Violet said thoughtfully. "To shoot down the crows, so V.F.D. can never get the sugar bowl."

"And that's why either Frank or Ernest had me hang birdpaper outside the window of the sauna," Klaus said. "If the crows are hit with the harpoon gun, they'll fall onto the birdpaper, and he'll know that the delivery had been unsuccessful."

"But was it Frank who had you lay out the birdpaper," Violet asked, "or Ernest? If it was Frank, then the birdpaper will serve as a signal to volunteers that they have been defeated. And if it was Ernest, then the birdpaper will serve as a signal to villains that they have triumphed."

"And what about the sugar bowl?" Klaus asked. "The crows will drop the sugar bowl if the harpoon hits them." He frowned at a page of his commonplace book. "If the crows drop a heavy object like that," he said, "it will fall straight down into the pond."

"Maybe no," Sunny said.

"Where else could it land?" Violet said.

"Spynsickle," Sunny said, which was her way of saying "laundry room."

"How would it get into the laundry room?" Klaus asked.

"The funnel," Sunny said. "Frank said. Or Ernest."

"So they had you place a lock on the laundry room door," Violet said, "so that nobody could get to the sugar bowl."

"But did Frank have Sunny activate the lock," Klaus asked, "or Ernest? If it was Frank, then the sugar bowl is locked away from any villains who want to get their hands on it. But if it was Ernest, then the sugar bowl is locked away from any volunteers who ought to get their hands on it."

"J. S.," Sunny said.

"J. S. is the key to the entire mystery," Violet agreed. "Esmé Squalor thinks J. S. is spoiling the party. Sir thinks J. S. is hosting the party. Hal thinks J. S. might be here to help. Kit thinks J. S. might be an enemy. And we still don't even know if J. S. is a man or a woman!"

"Like blind men," Sunny said, "with elephant."

"We have to find J. S.," Klaus agreed, "but

how? Trying to locate one guest in an enormous hotel is like finding one book in a library."

"A library without a catalog," Violet said quietly, and the three Baudelaires exchanged sad glances by the light of the frog-shaped lamp. The children had uncovered countless secrets in libraries under the most desperate of circumstances. They had decoded a message in a library while a hurricane raged outside, and had found important information while a sinister person chased them around a library in wicked shoes. They had discovered crucial facts in a library that held only three books, and obtained a vital map in a library that was only a pile of papers hidden underneath a table. The Baudelaires had even found the answers they were looking for in a library that had burned down, leaving only a few scraps of paper and a motto etched on an iron archway. Violet, Klaus, and Sunny stood for a moment at the concierge desk and thought of all the libraries they had seen, and wondered if any of the secrets they had uncovered would help

them find what they were looking for in the perplexing library of the Hotel Denouement.

"The world is quiet here," Sunny said,
reciting the motto her siblings had found, and
as her words echoed in the lobby, they heard a
noise above them, a quiet shuffling from the
enormous dome, scarcely audible over the
sound of the croaking frogs. The shuffling grew
louder, but the Baudelaires could not see anything in the blackness over their heads, which
was as dark as a crow flying through a pitch
black night. Finally, Violet lifted the frog-
shaped lamp as far as its cord would allow, and
all three children removed their sunglasses.
Faintly, they could see a shadowy shape lowering itself from the machinery of the clock using
what looked like a thick rope. It was an eerie
sight, like a spider lowering itself to the center
of a web, but the Baudelaires could not help but
admire the skill with which it was done. With
only a slight shuffle, the shape drew closer and
closer, until at last the children could see it was

a man, tall and skinny, with his legs and arms sticking out at odd angles, as if he were made of drinking straws instead of flesh and bone. The man was climbing down a rope he was unraveling at the same time, which is an activity I do not recommend unless you've had the proper training, and unfortunately the best trainer has been forced to go into hiding ever since a certain mountain headquarters was destroyed by arson, and he now earns his living doing spider imitations in a traveling show. Finally, the man was quite close to the ground, and with an elegant flourish he let go of the rope and landed silently on the floor. Then he strode toward the Baudelaires, pausing only to brush a speck of dust off the word MANAGER which was printed in fancy script over one of the pockets of his coat.

"Good evening, Baudelaires," the man said. "Forgive me for not revealing myself earlier, but I had to be sure that you were who I thought you were. It must have been very confusing to wander around this hotel without a catalog to help you."

"So there *is* a catalog?" Klaus asked.

"Of course there's a catalog," the man said. "You don't think I'd organize this entire building according to the Dewey Decimal System and then neglect to add a catalog, do you?"

"But where is the catalog?" Violet asked.

The man smiled. "Come outside," he said, "and I'll show you."

"Trap," Sunny murmured to her siblings, who nodded in agreement. "We're not following you," Violet said, "until we know that you're someone we can trust."

The man smiled. "I don't blame you for being suspicious," he said. "When I used to meet your father, Baudelaires, we would recite the work of an American humorist poet of the nineteenth century, so we could recognize one another in our disguises." He stopped in the middle of the lobby, and with a gesture from one of his odd, skinny arms, he began to recite a poem:

"So oft in theologic wars,
The disputants, I ween,
Rail on in utter ignorance
Of what each other mean,
And prate about an Elephant
Not one of them has seen!"

The words of the American humorist poets of the nineteenth century are often confusing, as they are liable to use such terms as "oft," which is a nineteenth-century abbreviation for "often"; "disputants," which refers to people who are arguing; "ween," which means "think"; and "rail on," which means to bicker for hours on end, the way you might do with a family member who is particularly bossy. Such poets might use the word "prate," which means "chatter," and they might spend an entire stanza discussing "theologic wars," a term which refers to arguing over what different people believe, the way you might also do with a family member who is particularly bossy. Even the Baudelaires, who'd had the works of American humorist poets of the nineteenth century recited to them many times over their childhood, had trouble understanding everything in the stanza, which simply made the point that all of the blind men in the poem were arguing pointlessly. But Violet, Klaus, and Sunny did not need to know exactly what the stanza meant. They only needed to know who wrote it.

"John Godfrey Saxe," said Sunny with a smile.

"Very good," the man said, and he walked across the shiny, silent floor of the lobby, pulling the rope down from the ceiling and tucking it into his belt.

"And who are you?" Violet called.

"Can't you guess?" the man asked, pausing at the large, curved entrance. The Baudelaires hurried to catch up with him as he turned to exit the hotel.

"Frank?" Klaus said.

"No," the man said, and began to walk down

the stairs. The Baudelaires took a step outside, where the croaking of the frogs in the pond was considerably louder, although the children could not see the pond through the cloud of steam coming from the funnel. Violet, Klaus, and Sunny looked at one another cautiously, and then began to follow.

"Ernest?" Sunny asked.

The man smiled, and kept walking down the stairs, disappearing into the steam. "No," he said, and the Baudelaire orphans stepped out of the hotel and disappeared along with him.

CHAPTER
Eight

The word "denouement" is not only the name of a hotel or the family who manages it, particularly nowadays, when the hotel and all its secrets have almost been forgotten, and the surviving members of the family have changed their names and are working in smaller, less glamorous inns. "Denouement" comes from the French, who use the word to describe the act of untying a knot, and it refers to the unraveling

of a confusing or mysterious story, such as the lives of the Baudelaire orphans, or anyone else you know whose life is filled with unanswered questions. The denouement is the moment when all of the knots of a story are untied, and all the threads are unraveled, and everything is laid out clearly for the world to see. But the denouement should not be confused with the end of a story. The denouement of "Snow White," for instance, occurs at the moment when Ms. White wakes up from her enchanted sleep, and decides to leave the dwarves behind and marry the handsome prince, and the mysterious old woman who gave her an apple has been exposed as the treacherous queen, but the end of "Snow White" occurs many years later, when a horseback riding accident plunges Ms. White into a fever from which she never recovers. The denouement of "Goldilocks and the Three Bears" occurs at the moment when the bears return home to find Goldilocks napping on their private property, and either chase her away from the premises, or eat her, depending on which version you have in your library, but the end of "Goldilocks and the Three Bears" occurs when a troop of young scouts neglect to extinguish their campfire and even the efforts of a volunteer fire department cannot save most of the wildlife from certain death. There are some stories in which the denouement and the end occur simultaneously, such as *La Forza del Destino*, in which the characters recognize and destroy one another over the course of a single song, but usually the denouement of a story is not the last event in the heroes' lives, or the last trouble that befalls them. It is often the second-to-last event, or the penultimate peril. As the Baudelaire orphans followed the mysterious man out of the hotel and through the cloud of steam to the edge of the reflective pond, the denouement of their story was fast approaching, but the end of their story still waited for them, like a secret still covered in fog, or a distant island in the midst of a troubled sea, whose waves raged against the shores of a city and the walls of a perplexing hotel.

"You must have thousands of questions, Baudelaires," said the man. "And just think—right here is where they can be answered."

"Who are you?" Violet asked.

"I'm Dewey Denouement," Dewey Denouement replied. "The third triplet. Haven't you heard of me?"

"No," Klaus said. "We thought there were only Frank and Ernest."

"Frank and Ernest get all the attention," Dewey said. "They get to walk around the hotel managing everything, while I just hide in the shadows and wind the clock." He gave the Baudelaires an enormous sigh, and scowled into the depths of the pond. "That's what I don't like about V.F.D.," he said. "All the smoke and mirrors."

"Smoke?" Sunny asked.

"'Smoke and mirrors,'" Klaus explained, "means 'trickery used to cover up the truth.'

But what does that have to do with V.F.D.?"

"Before the schism," Dewey said, "V.F.D. was like a public library. Anyone could join us and have access to all of the information we'd acquired. Volunteers all over the globe were reading each other's research, learning of each other's observations, and borrowing each other's books. For a while it seemed as if we might keep the whole world safe, secure, and smart."

"It must have been a wonderful time," Klaus said.

"I scarcely remember it," Dewey said. "I was four years old when the schism began. I was scarcely tall enough to reach my favorite shelf in the family library—the books labeled 020. But one night, just as our parents were hanging balloons for our fifth birthday party, my brothers and I were taken."

"Taken where?" Violet asked.

"Taken by whom?" Sunny asked.

"I admire your curiosity," Dewey said. "The woman who took me said that one can remain alive long past the usual date of disintegration if one is unafraid of change, insatiable in intellectual curiosity, interested in big things, and happy in small ways. And she took me to a place high in the mountains, where she said such things would be encouraged."

Klaus opened his commonplace book and began to take furious notes. "The headquarters," Klaus said, "in the Valley of Four Drafts."

"Your parents must have missed you," Violet said.

"They perished that very night," Dewey said, "in a terrible fire. I don't have to tell you how badly I felt when I learned the news."

The Baudelaires sighed, and looked out at the pond. Here and there on its calm surface they could see the reflections of a few lights in the windows, but most of the hotel was dark, so most of the pond was dark, too. The triplet, of course, did not have to tell the Baudelaires how it felt to lose one's parents so suddenly, or at such a young age. "It was not always this way, Baudelaires,"

Dewey said. "Once there were safe places scattered across the globe, and so orphans like yourselves did not have to wander from place to place, trying to find noble people who could be of assistance. With each generation, the schism gets worse. If justice does not prevail, soon there will be no safe places left, and nobody left to remember how the world ought to be."

"I don't understand," Violet said. "Why weren't we taken, like you?"

"You were," Dewey said. "You were taken into the custody of Count Olaf. And he tried to keep you in his custody, no matter how many noble people intervened."

"But why didn't anyone tell us what was going on?" Klaus asked. "Why did we have to figure things out all by ourselves?"

"I'm afraid that's the wicked way of the world," Dewey said, with a shake of his head. "Everything's covered in smoke and mirrors, Baudelaires. Since the schism, all the research, all the observations, even all of the books have been scattered all over the globe. It's like the elephant in the poem your father loved. Everyone has their hands on a tiny piece of the truth, but nobody can see the whole thing. Very soon, however, all that will change."

"Thursday," Sunny said.

"Exactly," Dewey said, smiling down at the youngest Baudelaire. "At long last, all of the noble people will be gathered together, along with all the research they've done, all the observations they've made, all the evidence they've collected, and all the books they've read. Just as a library catalog can tell you where a certain book is located, this catalog can tell you the location and behavior of every volunteer and every villain." He gestured to the hotel. "For years," he said, "while noble people wandered the world observing treachery, my comrade and I have been right here gathering all the information together. We've copied every note from every commonplace book from every volunteer and compiled it all into a catalog. Occasionally, when volunteers have been lost or safe places destroyed, we've had to go ourselves to collect the information that has been left behind. We've retrieved Josephine Anwhistle's files from Lake Lachrymose and carefully copied down their contents. We've pasted together the burnt scraps of Madame Lulu's archival library and taken notes on what we've found. We've searched the childhood home of the man with a beard but no hair, and interviewed the math teacher of the woman with hair but no beard. We've memorized important articles within the stacks of newspaper in Paltryville, and we've thrown important items out of the windows of our destroyed headquarters, so they might wind up somewhere safe at sea. We've taken every crime, every theft, every wicked deed, and every incident of rudeness since the schism began, and cataloged them into an entire library of misfortune. Eventually, every crucial secret ends up in my catalog. It's been my life's work. It has not been an easy life, but it has been an informative one."

"You're more than a volunteer," Violet said. "You're a librarian."

"I'm more of a sub-sub-librarian," Dewey said modestly. "That's what your parents used to call me, because my library work has been largely undercover and underground. Every villain in the world would want to destroy all this evidence, so it's been necessary to hide my life's work away."

"But where could you hide something that enormous?" Klaus said. "It would be like hiding an elephant. A catalog that immense would have to be as big as the hotel itself."

"It is," Dewey said, with a sly expression on his face. "In fact, it's *exactly* as big as the hotel."

Violet and Klaus turned their gaze from Dewey to look at each other in confusion, but Sunny was gazing neither at the sub-sub-librarian nor at her siblings, but down at the dark surface of the pond. "¡ahA" she said, pointing a small, gloved finger at the calm, still water.

"Exactly," Dewey said. "The truth has been right under everyone's noses, if anyone cared to look past the surface. Volunteers and villains alike know that the last safe place is the Hotel Denouement, but no one has ever questioned why the sign is written backward. They're staying in the TИƎMƎUOИƎD ꓶƎTOH, while the *real* last safe place—the catalog—is hidden safely at the bottom of the pond, in underwater rooms organized in a mirror image of the hotel itself. Our enemies could burn the entire building to the ground, but the most important secrets would be safe."

"But if the location of the catalog is such an important secret," Violet said, "why are you telling us?"

"Because you should know," Dewey said. "You've wandered the world, observing more villainy and gathering more evidence than most people do in a lifetime. I'm sure the observations and evidence you've gathered in your commonplace book will be valuable contributions to the catalog. Who better than you to keep the world's most important secrets?" He looked out at the pond, and then at each orphan in turn. "After Thursday," he continued, "you won't have to be at sea anymore, Baudelaires." The children knew that by the expression "at sea" he meant "lost and confused," and hearing those words brought tears to their eyes. "I hope you decide to make this your permanent home. I need someone with an inventive imagination who can improve on the aquatic design of the catalog. I need someone with the sort of research skills that can expand the catalog until it is the finest in the world. And, of course, we'll need to eat, and I've heard wonderful things about Sunny's cooking."

"Efcharisto," Sunny said modestly.

"Hal's meals are atrocious, I'm afraid," Dewey said with a rueful smile. "I don't know why he insisted on opening his restaurant in Room 954, when so many other suitable rooms were available. Bad food of any style is unpleasant, but bad Indian food is possibly the worst."

"Hal is a volunteer?" Klaus asked, remembering what Sunny had observed during her errands as a concierge.

"In a manner of speaking," Dewey said, using an expression which here means "sort of." "After the fire that destroyed Heimlich Hospital, my comrade arrived on the scene to catalog any information that might have survived. She found Hal in a very distraught condition. His Library of Records was in shambles, and he had nowhere to live. She offered him a position at the Hotel Denouement, where he might aid us in our research and learn to cook. Unfortunately he's only been good at one of those things."

"And what about Charles?" Violet asked, remembering what Klaus had observed during his errands.

"Charles has been searching for you since you left the lumbermill," Dewey said. "He cares for you, Baudelaires, despite the selfish and dreadful behavior of his partner. You've seen your share of wicked people, Baudelaires, but you've seen your share of people as noble as you are."

"I'm not sure we *are* noble," Klaus said quietly, flipping the pages of his commonplace book. "We caused those accidents at the lumbermill. We're responsible for the destruction of the hospital. We helped start the fire that destroyed Madame Lulu's archival library. We—"

"Enough," Dewey interrupted gently, putting a hand on Klaus's shoulder. "You're noble enough, Baudelaires. That's all we can ask for in this world."

The middle Baudelaire hung his head, so he was leaning against the sub-sub-librarian, and his sisters huddled against him, and all four volunteers stood for a moment silently in the dark. Tears fell from the eyes of the orphans— all four of them—and, as with many tears shed at night, they could not have said exactly why they were crying, although I know why I am

crying as I type this, and it is not because of the
onions that someone is slicing in the next room,
or because of the wretched curry he is planning
on making with them. I am crying because
Dewey Denouement was wrong. He was not
wrong when he said the Baudelaires were noble
enough, although I suppose many people might
argue about such a thing, if they were sitting
around a room together without a deck of cards
or something good to read. Dewey was wrong
when he said that being noble enough is all we
can ask for in this world, because we can ask for
much more than that. We can ask for a second
helping of pound cake, even though someone
has made it quite clear that we will not get any.
We can ask for a new watercolor set, even
though it will be pointed out that we never used
the old one, and that all of the paints dried into
a crumbly mess. We can ask for Japanese fight-
ing fish, to keep us company in our bedroom,
and we can ask for a special camera that will
allow us to take photographs even in the dark,

for obvious reasons, and we can ask for an extra sugar cube in our coffees in the morning and an extra pillow in our beds at night. We can ask for justice, and we can ask for a handkerchief, and we can ask for cupcakes, and we can ask for all the soldiers in the world to lay down their weapons and join us in a rousing chorus of "Cry Me a River," if that happens to be our favorite song. But we can also ask for something we are much more likely to get, and that is to find a person or two, somewhere in our travels, who will tell us that we are noble enough, whether it is true or not. We can ask for someone who will say, "You are noble enough," and remind us of our good qualities when we have forgotten them, or cast them into doubt. Most of us, of course, have parents and friends who tell us such things, after we have lost a badminton tournament or failed to capture a notorious counterfeiter who we discovered aboard a certain motorboat. But the Baudelaire orphans, of course, had no living parents, and their closest friends were high in the sky, in a self-sustaining hot air mobile home, battling eagles and a terrible henchman who had hooks instead of hands, so the acquaintance of Dewey Denouement, and the comforting words he had uttered, were a blessing. The Baudelaires stood with the sub-sub-librarian, grateful for this blessing, and at the sound of an approaching automobile, they looked to see two more blessings arriving via taxi, and were grateful all over again.

"Baudelaires!" called a familiar voice.

"Baudelaires!" called another one.

The siblings peered through the dark at the two figures emerging from the taxi, scarcely able to believe their eyes. These people were wearing strange eyeglasses made of two large cones that were attached to their heads with a mass of tangled rope, which was coiled up on top of their heads. Such glasses might have concealed the identity of the people who were wearing them, but the Baudelaires had no trouble recognizing the people who were hurrying toward them, even though they had not seen either person for a very long time, and had thought they would never see them again.

"Justice Strauss!" Violet cried.

"Jerome Squalor!" Klaus cried.

"J. S.!" Sunny cried.

"I'm so happy to find you," said the judge, taking off her Vision Furthering Device so she could dab at her eyes and embrace the children one by one. "I was afraid I'd never see you again. I'll never forgive myself for letting that idiotic banker take you away from me."

"And I'll never forgive myself," said Jerome, who had the misfortune of being married to Esmé Squalor, "for walking away from you children. I'm afraid I wasn't a very good guardian."

"And I'm afraid I wasn't a guardian at all," Justice Strauss said. "As soon as you were taken away in that automobile, I knew I had done the wrong thing, and when I heard the dreadful news about Dr. Montgomery I began searching for you. Eventually I found other people who were also trying to battle the wicked villains of this world, but I always hoped I would find you myself, if only to say how sorry I was."

"I'm sorry, too," Jerome said. "As soon as I heard about all the troubles that befell you in the Village of Fowl Devotees, I began my own Baudelaire search. Volunteers were leaving me messages everywhere—at least, I thought the messages were addressed to me."

"And I thought they were addressed to *me*," Justice Strauss said. "There are certainly plenty of people with the initials J. S."

"I began to feel like an impostor," Jerome said.

"You're not impostors," Dewey said. "You're volunteers." He turned to the Baudelaires. "Both these people have helped us immeasurably," he said, using a word which here means "a whole lot." "Justice Strauss has reported the details of your case to the other judges in the High Court. And Jerome Squalor has done some critical research on injustice."

"I was inspired by my wife," Jerome confessed, removing his Vision Furthering Device. "Wherever I looked for you, Baudelaires, I found selfish plots to steal your fortune. I read books on injustice in all the libraries you left behind and eventually wrote a book myself. *Odious Lusting After Finance* chronicles the history of greedy villains, treacherous girlfriends, bungling bankers, and all the other people responsible for injustice."

"No matter what we do, however," Justice Strauss said, "we can't erase the wrongs we did you, Baudelaires."

"She's right," Jerome Squalor said. "We should have been as noble as you are."

"You're noble enough," Violet said, and her siblings nodded in agreement, as the judge and the injustice expert embraced them again. When someone has disappointed you, as Justice Strauss and Jerome Squalor disappointed the Baudelaires, it is often difficult to decide whether to continue their acquaintance, even if the disappointers have done noble things in the meantime. There are some who say that you should forgive everyone, even the people who have disappointed you immeasurably. There are others who say you should not forgive anyone, and should stomp off in a huff no matter how many times they apologize. Of these two philosophies, the second one is of course much more fun, but it can also grow exhausting to stomp off in a huff every time someone has disappointed you, as everyone disappoints everyone eventually, and one can't stomp off in a huff every minute of the day. When the Baudelaires thought about the harm that each J. S. had done to them, it was as if they had gotten a bruise quite some time ago, one that had mostly faded but that still hurt when they touched it, and when they touched this bruise it made them want to stomp off in a huff. But on that evening—or, more properly, very early Wednesday morning—the siblings did not want to stomp off into the hotel, where so many wicked people were gathered, or into the pond, which was likely to be very cold and clammy at this time of night. They wanted to forgive these two adults, and to embrace them, despite their disappointment.

"I don't mean to break up all this embracing," Dewey said, "but we have work to do, volunteers. As one of the first volunteers said a very long time ago, 'Though boys throw stones at frogs in sport, the frogs do not die in sport, but in earnest.'"

"Speaking of frogs," Justice Strauss said, "I'm afraid to report that we couldn't see a thing from the other side of the pond. These Vision Furthering Devices work well in the daytime, but looking through special sunglasses after sunset makes everything look as dark as a crow flying through a pitch black night—which is precisely what we're looking for."

"Justice Strauss is correct," Jerome said sadly. "We couldn't verify the arrival of the crows, or whether their journey was interrupted."

"We couldn't see if even a single crow was trapped," the judge said, "or if the sugar bowl fell into the funnel."

"Funnel?" Dewey repeated.

"Yes," Justice Strauss said. "You told us that if our enemies shot down the crows, they would have fallen onto the birdpaper."

"And if the crows fell onto the birdpaper," Jerome continued, "then the sugar bowl would drop into the laundry room, right?"

Dewey looked slyly at the steaming funnel, and then at the surface of the pond. "So it would appear," he said. "Our enemies capturing the sugar bowl would be as troubling as their capture of the Medusoid Mycelium."

"So you already know about the plan to shoot down the crows, and capture the sugar bowl?" Violet said incredulously.

"Yes," Dewey said. "Justice Strauss learned that the harpoon gun had been taken up to the rooftop sunbathing salon. Jerome noticed that birdpaper was dangling out of the window of the sauna in Room 613. And I gave Sunny the lock myself, so she could lock up the laundry in Room 025."

"You know about all the villainous people who are lurking in the hotel?" Klaus said, equally incredulously.

"Yes," Justice Strauss said. "We observed rings on all the wooden furniture, from people refusing to use coasters. Obviously there are many villains staying in the hotel."

"Mycelium?" Sunny asked, with perhaps just a touch more incredulousness than her siblings.

"Yes," Jerome said. "We've learned that Olaf has managed to acquire a few spores locked tight in a diving helmet."

The Baudelaires looked at the commonplace book in Klaus's hands, and then back at the sub-sub-librarian. "I guess our observations and evidence aren't such valuable contributions after all," Violet said. "All the mysteries we encountered in the hotel had already been solved."

"It doesn't matter, Baudelaires," Jerome said. "Olaf won't dare unleash the Medusoid Mycelium unless he gets his hands on the sugar bowl, and he'll never find it."

"I'm the only one who knows which words will unlock the Vernacularly Fastened Door," Dewey said, ushering the children back toward the entrance of the hotel, "and there's not a villainous person on Earth who has done enough reading to guess them before Thursday. By then, all of the volunteers will present the research they've done on Count Olaf and his associates to the prosecution, and all their treachery will finally end."

"Jerome Squalor will be an important witness," Justice Strauss said. "His comprehensive history of injustice will help the High Court reach a verdict."

"Prosecution?" Violet asked.

"Witness?" Klaus asked.

"Verdict?" Sunny said.

The three adults smiled at one another, and

then at the Baudelaires. "That's what we've been trying to tell you," Dewey said gently. "V.F.D. has researched an entire catalog of Olaf's treachery. On Thursday, Justice Strauss and the other judges of the High Court will hear from each and every one of our volunteers. Count Olaf, Esmé Squalor, and all of the other villainous people gathered here will finally be brought to justice."

"You'll never have to hide from Olaf again," Jerome said, "or worry that anyone will steal your fortune."

"We just have to wait for tomorrow, Baudelaires," Justice Strauss said, "and your troubles will finally be over."

"It's like my comrade always says," Dewey said. "Right, temporarily defeated, is stronger than evil triumphant."

Wrong! The clanging of the clock announced that it was one in the morning, and without another word, Dewey took Violet's hand, and Justice Strauss took Klaus's, and Jerome Squalor leaned down and took Sunny's hand, and the three adults led the three orphans up the stairs toward the hotel's entrance, walking past the taxi, which still sat there, engine purring, with the figure of the driver just a shadow in the window. The three adults smiled at the children, and the children smiled back, but of course the Baudelaires were not born yesterday, an expression which means "young or innocent enough to believe things certain people say about the world." If the Baudelaires had been born yesterday, perhaps they would be innocent enough to believe that all of their troubles were truly about to end, and that Count Olaf and all of his treacherous associates would be judged by the High Court, and condemned to the proper punishment for all their ignoble deeds, and that the children would spend the rest of their days working with Dewey Denouement on his enormous underwater catalog, if they only waited for tomorrow. But the three siblings were not born yesterday. Violet was born more than fifteen years before this particular Wednesday, and Klaus was born approximately two years after that, and even Sunny, who had just passed out of babyhood, was not born yesterday. Neither were you, unless of course I am wrong, in which case welcome to the world, little baby, and congratulations on learning to read so early in life. But if you were not born yesterday, and you have read anything about the Baudelaire children's lives, then you cannot be surprised that this happy moment was almost immediately cut short by the appearance of a most unwelcome person at the moment the children were led through the fog of steam coming from the laundry room funnel and through the entrance of the Hotel Denouement as the one loud *Wrong!* faded into nothing. This person was standing in the center of the lobby, his tall lean body bent into a theatrical pose as if he were waiting for a crowd to applaud, and you will not be surprised to know what was tattooed on his ankle, which the children could see poking out of a hole in his sock even in the dim light of the room. You were not born yesterday, probably, so you will not be surprised to find that this notorious villain had reappeared in the Baudelaires' lives for the penultimate time, and the Baudelaires were also not born yesterday, and so they also were not surprised. They were not born yesterday, but when Count Olaf turned to face them, and gazed upon them with his shiny, shiny eyes, the Baudelaire orphans wished they had not been born at all.

"Ha!" Count Olaf shrieked, pointing at the Baudelaire orphans with a bony finger, and the children were thankful for small mercies. A small mercy is simply a tiny thing that has gone right in a world gone wrong, like a sprig of delicious parsley next to a spoiled tuna sandwich, or a lovely dandelion in a garden that is being devoured by vicious goats. A small mercy, like a small flyswatter, is unlikely to be of any real

help, but nevertheless the three siblings, even in their horror and disgust at seeing Olaf again, were thankful for the small mercy that the villain had apparently lost interest in his new laugh. The last time the Baudelaires had seen the villain, he'd been aboard a strange submarine shaped like an octopus, and he'd developed a laugh that was equally strange, full of snorts and squeaks and words that happened to begin with the letter H. But as the villain strode toward the children and the adults who were clutching their hands, it was clear he had since adopted a style of laughter that was succinct, a word which here means "only the word 'ha.'" "Ha!" he cried. "I knew I'd find you orphans again! Ha! And now you're in my clutches! Ha!"

"We're not in your clutches," Violet said. "We just happen to be standing in the same room."

"That's what you think, orphan," Olaf

sneered. "I'm afraid the man who's holding your hand is one of my associates. Hand her over, Ernest. Ha!"

"Ha yourself, Olaf," said Dewey Denouement. His voice was firm and confident, but Violet felt his hand trembling in hers. "I'm not Ernest, and I'm not handing her over!"

"Well, then hand her over, Frank!" Olaf said. "You might consider doing your hair differently so I can tell you apart."

"I'm not Frank, either," Dewey said.

"You can't fool me!" Count Olaf growled. "I wasn't born yesterday, you know! You're one of those idiotic twins! I should know! Thanks to me, you two are the only survivors of the entire family!"

"Triplets run in my family," Dewey said, "not twins. I'm Dewey Denouement."

At this, Count Olaf's one eyebrow raised in astonishment. "Dewey Denouement," he murmured. "So you're a real person! I always thought you were a legendary figure, like unicorns or Giuseppe Verdi."

"Giuseppe Verdi is not a legendary figure," Klaus said indignantly. "He's an operatic composer!"

"Silence, bookworm!" Olaf ordered. "Children should not speak while adults are arguing! Hand over the orphans, adults!"

"Nobody's handing over the Baudelaires!" Justice Strauss said, clutching Klaus's hand. "You have no legal right to them or their fortune!"

"You can't just grab children as if they were pieces of fruit in a bowl!" Jerome Squalor cried. "It's injustice, and we won't have it!"

"You'd better watch yourselves," Count Olaf said, narrowing his shiny eyes. "I have associates lurking everywhere in this hotel."

"So do we," Dewey said. "Many volunteers have arrived early, and within hours the streets will be flooded with taxis carrying noble people here to this hotel."

"How can you be sure they're noble people?"

Count Olaf asked. "A taxi will pick up anyone who signals for one."

"These people are associates of ours," Dewey said fiercely. "They won't fail us."

"Ha!" Count Olaf said. "You can't rely on associates. More comrades have failed me than I can count. Why, Hooky and Fiona double-crossed me just yesterday, and let you brats escape! Then they double-crossed me again and stole my submarine!"

"We can rely on our friends," Violet said quietly, "more than you can rely on yours."

"Is that so?" Count Olaf asked, and leaned toward the children with a ravenous smile. "Have you learned nothing after all your adventures?" he asked. "Every noble person has failed you, Baudelaires. Why, look at the idiots standing next to you! A judge who let me marry you, a man who gave up on you altogether, and a sub-sub-librarian who spends his life sneaking around taking notes. They're hardly a noble bunch."

"Charles is here, from Lucky Smells Lumbermill," Klaus said. "He cares about us."

"Sir is here," Olaf retorted. "He doesn't. Ha!"

"Hal," Sunny said.

"Vice Principal Nero and Mr. Remora," Olaf replied, counting each nasty person on his filthy fingers. "And that pesky little reporter from *The Daily Punctilio*, who's here to write silly articles praising my cocktail party. And ridiculous Mr. Poe, who arrived just hours ago to investigate a bank robbery. Ha!"

"Those people don't count," Klaus said. "They're not associates of yours."

"They might as well be," Count Olaf replied. "They've been an enormous help. And every second, more associates of mine get closer and closer."

"So do our friends," Violet said. "They're flying across the sea as we speak, and by tomorrow, their self-sustaining hot air mobile home will land on the roof."

"Only if they've managed to survive my eagles," Count Olaf said with a growl.

"They will," Klaus said. "Just like we've survived you."

"And how did you survive me?" Olaf asked. "*The Daily Punctilio* is full of your crimes. You lied to people. You stole. You abandoned people in danger. You set fires. Time after time you've relied on treachery to survive, just like everyone else. There are no truly noble people in this world."

"Our parents," Sunny said fiercely.

Count Olaf looked surprised that Sunny had spoken, and then gave all three Baudelaires a smile that made them shudder. "I guess the sub-sub-librarian hasn't told you the story about your parents," he said, "and a box of poison darts. Why don't you ask him, orphans? Why don't you ask this legendary librarian about that fateful evening at the opera?"

The Baudelaires turned to look at Dewey, who had begun to blush. But before they could ask him anything, they were interrupted by a voice coming from a pair of sliding doors that had quietly opened.

"Don't ask him that," Esmé Squalor said. "I have a much more important question."

With a mocking laugh, the treacherous girl-friend emerged from the elevator, her silver sandals clumping on the floor and her lettuce leaves rustling against her skin. Behind her was Carmelita Spats, who was still wearing her ballplaying cowboy superhero soldier pirate outfit and carrying the harpoon gun Violet had delivered, and behind her three more people emerged from the elevator. First came the attendant from the rooftop sunbathing salon, still wearing green sunglasses and a long, baggy robe. Following the attendant was the mysteri-ous chemist from outside the sauna, dressed in a long, white coat and a surgical mask, and last out of the elevator was the washerwoman from the laundry room, with long, blond hair and rumpled clothing. The Baudelaires recognized these people from their observations as flaneurs, but then the attendant removed his robe to reveal his back, which had a small hump on the shoulder, and the chemist removed her surgical mask, not with one of her hands but with one of her feet, and the washerwoman removed a long, blond wig with both hands at the exact same time, and the three siblings recognized the three henchfolk all over again.

"Hugo!" cried Violet.

"Colette!" cried Klaus.

"Kevin!" cried Sunny.

"Esmé!" cried Jerome.

"Why isn't anybody calling out my name?" demanded Carmelita, stomping one of her bright blue boots. She pranced toward Violet, who observed that two of the four long, sharp hooks were missing from the weapon. This sort of observation may be important for a flaneur, but it is dreadful for any reader of this book, who probably does not want to know where the remaining harpoons will end up. "I'm a ballplaying cowboy superhero soldier pirate," she crowed to the oldest Baudelaire, "and you're nothing but a cakesniffer. Call my name or I'll shoot you with this harpoon gun!"

"Carmelita!" Esmé said, her silver mouth twisting into an expression of shock. "Don't point that gun at Violet!"

"Esmé's right," Count Olaf said. "Don't waste the harpoons. We may need them."

"Yes!" Esmé cried. "There's always important work to do before a cocktail party, particularly if you want it to be the innest in the world! We need to put slipcovers on the couches, and hide our associates beneath them! We need to put vases of flowers on the piano and electric eels in the fountain! We need to hang streamers and volunteers from the ceiling! We need to play music, so people can dance, and block the exits, so they can't leave! And most of all, we have to cook in food and prepare in cocktails! Food and drink are the most important aspect of every social occasion, and our in recipes—"

"The most important aspect of every social occasion isn't food and drink!" Dewey interrupted indignantly. "It's conversation!"

"You're the one who should flee!" Justice Strauss said. "Your cocktail party will be canceled, due to the host and hostess being brought to justice by the High Court!"

"You're as foolish as you were when we were neighbors," Count Olaf said. "The High Court can't stop us. V.F.D. can't stop us. Hidden somewhere in this hotel is one of the most deadly fungi in the entire world. When Thursday comes, the fungus will come out of hiding and destroy everyone it touches! At last I'll be free to steal the Baudelaire fortune and perform any other act of treachery that springs to mind!"

"You won't dare unleash the Medusoid Mycelium," Dewey said. "Not while I have the sugar bowl."

"Funny you should mention the sugar bowl," Esmé Squalor said, although the Baudelaires could see she didn't think it was funny at all. "That's just what we want to ask you about."

"The sugar bowl?" Count Olaf asked, his eyes shining bright. "Where is it?"

"The freaks will tell you," Esmé said.

"It's true, boss," said Hugo. "I may be a mere hunchback, but I saw Carmelita shoot down the crows using the harpoon gun Violet brought her."

Justice Strauss turned to Violet in astonishment. "*You* gave Carmelita the harpoon gun?" she gasped.

"Well, yes," Violet said. "I had to perform concierge errands as part of my disguise."

"The harpoon gun was supposed to be kept away from villains," the judge said, "not given to them. Why didn't Frank stop you?"

Violet thought back to her unfathomable conversation with Frank. "I think he tried," she said quietly, "but I had to take the harpoon gun up to the roof. What else could I do?"

"I hit two crows!" bragged Carmelita Spats. "That means Countie has to teach me how to spit like a real ballplaying cowboy superhero soldier pirate!"

"Don't worry, darling," Esmé said. "He'll teach you. Won't you, Olaf?"

Count Olaf sighed, as if he had better things to do than teach a little girl how to propel saliva out of her mouth. "Yes, Carmelita," he said, "I'll teach you how to spit."

Colette took center stage, a phrase which here means "stepped forward, and twisted her body into an unusual shape." "Even a contortionist like me," she said, her mouth moving beneath her elbow, "could see what happened after Carmelita shot the crows. They fell right onto the birdpaper that Klaus dangled out the window."

"*You* dangled the birdpaper out the window?" Jerome asked the middle Baudelaire.

"Ernest told me to," Klaus said, finally realizing which manager had spoken to him in the sauna. "I had to obey him as part of my disguise."

"You can't just do what everyone tells you to do," Jerome said.

"What else could I do?" Klaus said.

"When the crows hit the birdpaper," Kevin said, gesturing with one hand and then the other, "they dropped the sugar bowl. I didn't see where it went with either my right eye or my left one, which I'm sad to say are equally strong. But I did see Sunny turn the door of the laundry room into a Vernacularly Fastened Door."

"Aha!" Count Olaf cried. "The sugar bowl must have fallen down the funnel!"

"I still don't see why I had to disguise myself as a washerwoman," Kevin said timidly. "I could have just been a washerperson, and not worn this humiliating wig."

"Or you could have been a noble person," Violet could not help adding, "instead of spying on a brave volunteer."

"What else could I do?" Kevin asked, shrugging both shoulders equally high.

"You could be a volunteer yourself," Klaus said, looking at all of his former carnival coworkers. "All of you could stand with us now, instead of helping Count Olaf with his schemes."

"I could never be a noble person," Hugo said sadly. "I have a hump on my back."

"And I'm a contortionist," Colette said. "Someone who can bend their body into unusual shapes could never be a volunteer."

"V.F.D. would never accept an ambidextrous person," Kevin said. "It's my destiny to be a treacherous person."

"Galimatias!" Sunny cried.

"Nonsense!" Dewey said, who understood at once what Sunny had said. "I'm ambidextrous myself, and I've managed to do something worthwhile with my life. Being treacherous isn't your destiny! It's your choice!"

"I'm glad you feel that way," Esmé Squalor said. "You have a choice this very moment, Frank. Tell me where the sugar bowl is, or else!"

"That's not a choice," Dewey said, "and I'm not Frank."

Esmé frowned. "Then you have a choice this very moment, Ernest. Tell me where the sugar bowl is, or—"

"Dewey," Sunny said.

Esmé blinked at the youngest Baudelaire, who noticed that the villainous woman's eyelashes had also been painted silver. "What?" she asked.

"It's true," Olaf said. "He's the real sub-sub. It turns out he's not legendary, like Verdi."

"Is that so?" Esmé Squalor said. "So someone has really been cataloging everything that has happened between us?"

"It's been my life's work," Dewey said. "Eventually, every crucial secret ends up in my catalog."

"Then you know all about the sugar bowl," Esmé said, "and what's inside. You know how important that thing was, and how many lives were lost in the quest to find it. You know how difficult it was to find a container that could hold it safely, securely, and attractively. You know what it means to the Baudelaires and what it means to the Snickets." She took one sandaled step closer to Dewey, and stretched out one silver fingernail—the one shaped like an S—until it was almost poking him in the eye. "And you know," she said in a terrible voice, "that it is *mine*."

"Not anymore," Dewey said.

"Beatrice stole it from *me*!" Esmé cried.

"There are worse things," Dewey said, "than theft."

At this, the girlfriend gave the sub-sub-librarian a chuckle that made the Baudelaires' blood run cold. "There certainly are," she said, and strode toward Carmelita Spats. With one spiky fingernail—the one shaped like an M—she moved the harpoon gun so it was pointing at the triplet. "Tell me how to open that door," she said, "or this little girl will harpoon you."

"I'm not a little girl!" Carmelita reminded

Esmé nastily. "I'm a ballplaying cowboy super-hero soldier pirate! And I'm not going to shoot any more harpoons until Countie teaches me how to spit."

"You'll do what we say, Carmelita," Olaf growled. "I already purchased that ridiculous outfit for you, and that boat for you to prowl the swimming pool. Point that weapon at Dewey this instant!"

"Teach me to spit!" Carmelita said.

"Point the weapon!"

"Teach me to spit!"

"Point the weapon!"

"Teach me to spit!"

"Weapon!"

"Spit!"

"Weapon!"

"Spit!"

With a raspy roar, Count Olaf roughly yanked the harpoon gun out of Carmelita's hands, knocking her to the floor. "I'll never teach you how to spit as long as I live!" he shouted. "Ha!"

"Darling!" Esmé gasped. "You can't break your promise to our darling little girl!"

"*I'm not a darling little girl!*" Carmelita screamed. "*I'm a ballplaying cowboy superhero soldier pirate!*"

"You're a spoiled baby!" Olaf corrected. "I never wanted a brat like you around anyway! It's about time you were shown some discipline!"

"But discipline is out!" Esmé said.

"I don't care what's out and what's in!" Count Olaf cried. "I'm tired of having a girl-friend obsessed with fashion! All you do is sit around rooftop sunbathing salons while I run around doing all the work!"

"If I hadn't been on the roof," Esmé retorted, "the sugar bowl would have been delivered to V.F.D.! Besides, I was guarding—"

"Never mind what you were doing," Olaf said. "You're fired!"

"You can't fire me!" Esmé growled. "I quit!"

"Well, you can leave by mutual agreement," Olaf grumbled, and then, with another succinct

"Ha!" he lifted the harpoon gun and pointed it at Dewey Denouement. "Tell us the three phrases we need to type into the lock in order to open the Vernacularly Fastened Door and search the laundry room!"

"You won't find anything in the laundry room," Dewey said, "except piles of dirty sheets, a few washing and drying machines, and some extremely flammable chemicals."

"I may have a handsome, youthful glow," Olaf snarled, "but I wasn't born yesterday! Ha! If there's nothing in the laundry room, why did you put a V.F.D. lock on the door?"

"Perhaps it's just a decoy," Dewey said, his hand still trembling in Violet's.

"Decoy?" Olaf said.

"'Decoy' is a word with several meanings," the triplet explained. "It can refer to a corner of a pond where ducks can be captured, or to an imitation of a duck or other animal used to attract a real specimen. Or, it can mean something used to distract people, such as a lock on a door that does not contain a certain sugar bowl."

"If the lock is a decoy, sub-sub," Count Olaf sneered, "then you won't mind telling me how to open it."

"Very well," Dewey said, still struggling to sound calm. "The first phrase is a description of a medical condition that all three Baudelaire children share."

The Baudelaires shared a smile.

"The second phrase is the weapon that left you an orphan, Olaf," Dewey said.

The Baudelaires shared a frown.

"And the third," Dewey said, "is the famous unfathomable question in the best-known novel by Richard Wright."

The Baudelaire sisters shared a look of confusion, and then looked hopefully at Klaus, who slowly shook his head.

"I don't have time to medically examine the Baudelaires," Olaf said, "or shove my face into any best-known novels!"

"Wicked people never have time for reading," Dewey said. "It's one of the reasons for their wickedness."

"I've had enough of your games!" Count Olaf roared. "Ha! If I don't hear the exact phrases used to open the lock by the time Esmé counts to ten, I'll fire the harpoon gun and tear you to shreds! Esmé, count to ten!"

"I'm not counting to ten," Esmé pouted. "I'm not going to do anything for you ever again!"

"I knew it!" Jerome said. "I knew you could be a noble person again, Esmé! You don't have to parade around in an indecent bikini in the middle of the night threatening sub-sub-librarians! You can stand with us, in the name of justice."

"Let's not go overboard," Esmé said. "Just because I'm dumping my boyfriend doesn't mean I'm going to be a goody-goody like you. Justice is out. Injustice is in. That's why it's called *in*justice."

"You should do what's right in this world," Justice Strauss said, "not just what's fashionable.

I understand your situation, Esmé. When I was your age, I spent years as a horse thief before realizing—"

"I don't want to hear your boring stories," Count Olaf snarled. "The only thing I want to hear are three exact phrases from Dewey's mouth, or his destiny will be death by harpoon, as soon as I say the number ten. *One!*"

"Stop!" Justice Strauss cried. "In the name of the law!"

"*Two!*"

"Stop!" Jerome Squalor pleaded. "In the name of injustice!"

"*Three!*"

"*Stop!*" Violet ordered, and her siblings nodded in fierce agreement. The Baudelaires realized, as I'm sure you have realized, that the adults standing with them were going to do nothing that would stop Count Olaf from reaching ten and pulling the trigger of the harpoon gun, and that Justice Strauss and Jerome Squalor would fail them, as so many noble people had failed them before. But the siblings also knew that this failure would not hurt them—at least, not right away. It would hurt Dewey Denouement, and without another word the three children dropped the hands of the adults and stood in front of the sub-sub-librarian, shielding him from harm.

"You can't harpoon this man," Klaus said to Count Olaf, scarcely believing what he was saying. "You'll have to harpoon us first."

"Or," Sunny said, "put down gun."

Dewey Denouement looked too amazed to speak, but Count Olaf merely turned his disdainful gaze from the sub-sub-librarian to the three children. "I wouldn't mind harpooning you either, orphans," he said, his eyes shining bright. "When it comes to slaughtering people, I'm very flexible! Ha! *Four!*"

Violet took a step toward the count, who was holding the harpoon gun so it pointed at her chest. "Lay down your weapon, Olaf," the eldest Baudelaire said. "You don't want to do this wicked thing."

Count Olaf blinked, but did not move the gun. "Of course I do," he said. "If the sub-sub doesn't tell me how to get the sugar bowl, I'll pull the trigger no matter who's standing in front of me! Ha! *Five!*"

Klaus took a step forward, joining his sister. "You have a choice," he said. "You can choose not to pull that trigger!"

"And you can choose death by harpoon!" Count Olaf cried. "*Six!*"

"Please," Sunny said, joining her siblings. The villain did not move, but standing together, the three Baudelaires walked closer and closer to the harpoon gun, shielding Dewey all the while.

"*Seven!*"

"*Please*," the youngest Baudelaire said again. The Baudelaires walked slowly but steadily toward the harpoon gun, their echoing footsteps the only sound in the silent lobby except for Olaf's shrieking of higher and higher numbers.

"*Eight!*"

They walked closer.

"*Nine!*"

The children took one last step, and silently put their hands on the harpoon gun, which felt ice cold, even through their white gloves. They tried to pull the weapon out of Olaf's hands, but their first guardian did not let go, and for a long moment the youngsters and the adult were gathered around the terrible weapon in silence. Violet stared at the hooked tip of one harpoon that was pressed against her chest. Klaus stared straight ahead at the bright red trigger that could press at any moment, and Sunny stared into Olaf's shiny, shiny eyes for even the smallest sign of nobility.

"What else can I do?" the villain asked, so quietly the children could not be sure they had heard him correctly.

"Give us the gun," Violet said. "It's not your destiny to do this treacherous deed."

"Give us the gun," Klaus said. "It's not your

destiny to be a wicked person."

"*La Forza del Destino*," Sunny said, and then nobody said anything more. It was so quiet in the lobby that the Baudelaires could hear Olaf draw breath as he got ready to shout the word "ten."

But then, in an instant, they heard another sound, specifically a very loud cough, and in an instant everything changed, which is the wicked way of the world. In an instant, you can light a match and start a fire that can destroy the lives of countless people. In an instant, you can remove a cake from the oven and provide dessert for countless others, assuming that the cake is very large, and the others are not very hungry. In an instant, you can change a few words in a poem by Robert Frost and communicate with your associates through a code known as Verse Fluctuation Declaration, and in an instant, you can realize where something is hidden and decide whether you are going to retrieve it or let it stay hidden, where it might

never be found and eventually be forgotten by
all but a few very well-read and very distraught
figures, who are themselves forgotten by all but
a few very well-read and very distraught figures,
who in turn are forgotten, and so on, and so on,
and so on, and a few more so ons besides. All
this can happen in an instant, as if a single
instant is an enormous container, capable of
holding countless secrets safely, securely, and
attractively, such as the countless secrets held
in the Hotel Denouement, or in the hidden
underwater catalog in its rippling reflection. But
in this instant, in the hotel's enormous lobby,
the Baudelaire orphans heard a cough, as loud
as it was familiar, and in this instant Count Olaf
turned to see who was walking into the lobby,
and hurriedly pushed the harpoon gun into the
Baudelaires' hands when he saw a figure wearing pajamas with drawings of money all over
them and a bewildered expression on his face.
In this instant, the three siblings grasped the
weapon, feeling its heavy, dark weight in their

hands, and in this instant the gun slipped from their hands and clattered to the green wooden floor, and in this instant they heard the red trigger *click!*, and in this instant the penultimate harpoon was fired with a *swoosh!* and sailed through the enormous, domed room and struck someone a fatal blow, a phrase which here means "killed one of the people in the room."

"What's going on?" Mr. Poe demanded, for it was not his destiny to be slain by a harpoon, at least not on this particular evening. "I could hear people arguing all the way from Room 174. What in the world—" and in that instant he stopped, and gazed in horror at the three siblings. "Baudelaires!" he gasped, but he was not the only person gasping. Violet gasped, and Klaus gasped, and Sunny gasped, and Justice Strauss and Jerome Squalor gasped, and Hugo, Colette, and Kevin—who were accustomed to violence from their days as carnival employees and as henchmen to a villain—gasped, and Carmelita Spats gasped, and Esmé Squalor gasped, and even Count Olaf gasped, although it is unusual for a villain to gasp unless he is discovering a crucial secret, or suffering very great pain. But it was Dewey Denouement who gasped loudest of all, louder even than the *Wrong!*s that thundered through the hotel as the clock struck two. *Wrong! Wrong!* the clock thundered, but all the Baudelaires heard was Dewey's pained, choking gasp, as he stumbled backward through the lobby, one hand on his chest, and the other clutching the tail end of the harpoon, which stuck out from his body at an odd angle, like a drinking straw, or a reflection of one of Dewey's skinny arms.

"*Dewey!*" Violet cried.

"*Dewey!*" Klaus cried.

"*Denouement!*" Sunny cried, but the sub-sub-librarian did not answer, and stumbled backward out of the hotel in silence. For a moment, the children were too shocked to move as they watched him disappear into the cloud of steam rising from the laundry room funnel, but then they ran after him, hurrying down the stairs as they heard a *splash!* from the edge of the pond. By the time the Baudelaires reached him, he was already beginning to sink, his trembling body making ripples in the water. There are those who say that the world is like a calm pond, and that anytime a person does even the smallest thing, it is as if a stone has dropped into the pond, spreading circles of ripples further and further out, until the entire world has been changed by one tiny action, but the Baudelaires could not bear to think of the tiny action of the trigger of the harpoon gun, or how the world had changed in just one instant. Instead, they frantically rushed to the edge of the pond as the sub-sub-librarian began to sink. Klaus grabbed one hand, and Sunny grabbed the other, and Violet reached for his face, as if she were comforting someone who had begun to cry.

"You'll be O.K.," Violet cried. "Let us get you out of the water."

Dewey shook his head, and then gave the

children a terrible frown, as if he were trying to speak but unable to find the words.

"You'll survive," Klaus said, although he knew, both from reading about dreadful events and from dreadful events in his own life, that this simply was not true.

Dewey shook his head again. By now, only his head was above the surface of the water, and his two trembling hands. The children could not see his body, or the harpoon, which was a small mercy.

"We failed you," Sunny said.

Dewey shook his head one more time, this time very wildly in violent disagreement. He opened his mouth, and reached one hand out of the water, pointing past the Baudelaires toward the dark, dark sky as he struggled to utter the word he most wanted to say. "Kit," he whispered finally, and then, slipping from the grasp of the children, he disappeared into the dark water, and the Baudelaire orphans wept alone for the mercies denied them, and for the wicked, wicked way of the world.

CHAPTER Ten

"*What* was that?" a voice called out.

"It sounded like a harpoon gun being fired!" cried another voice.

"A harpoon gun?" asked a third voice. "This is supposed to be a hotel, not a shooting gallery!"

"I heard a splash!" cried someone.

"Me too!" agreed someone else. "It sounded like

somebody fell into the pond!"

The Baudelaire orphans gazed at the settling surface of the pond and saw the reflections of shutters and windows opening on every story of the Hotel Denouement. Lights went on, and the silhouettes of people appeared, leaning out of the windows and pointing down at the weeping children, who were too upset to pay much attention to all the shouting.

"What's all this shouting about?" asked another voice. "I was fast asleep!"

"It's the middle of the night!" complained someone else. "Why is everybody yelling?"

"I'll tell you why there's yelling!" yelled someone. "Someone was shot with a harpoon gun and then fell into the pond!"

"Come back to bed, Bruce," said someone else.

"I can't sleep if there's murderers on the loose!" cried another guest.

"Amen, brother!" said another person. "If a crime has been committed, then it's our duty to stand around in our pajamas in the name of justice!"

"I can't sleep anyway!" said somebody. "That lousy Indian food has kept me up all night!"

"Somebody tell me what's going on!" called a voice. "The readers of *The Daily Punctilio* will want to know what's happened."

The sound of the voice of Geraldine Julienne, and the mention of her inaccurate publication, forced the children to stop crying, if only for a moment. They knew it would be wise to postpone their grief—a phrase which here means "mourn the death of Dewey Denouement at a later time"—and make sure that the newspaper printed the truth.

"There's been an accident," Violet called, not turning her eyes from the surface of the pond. "A terrible accident."

"One of the hotel managers has died," Klaus said.

"Which one?" asked a voice from a high window. "Frank or Ernest?"

"Dewey," Sunny said.

"There's no Dewey," said another voice. "That's a legendary figure."

"He's not a legendary figure!" Violet said indignantly. "He's a sub—"

Klaus put his hand on his sister's, and the eldest Baudelaire stopped talking. "Dewey's catalog is a secret," he whispered. "We can't have it announced in *The Daily Punctilio*."

"But truth," Sunny murmured.

"Klaus is right," Violet said. "Dewey asked us to keep his secret, and we can't fail him." She looked sadly out at the pond, and wiped the tears from her eyes. "It's the least we can do," she said.

"I didn't realize this was a sad occasion," said another hotel guest. "We should observe everything carefully, and intrude only if absolutely necessary."

"I disagree!" said someone in a raspy shout. "We should intrude right now, and observe only if absolutely necessary!"

"We should call the authorities!" said some-one else.

"We should call the manager!"

"We should call the concierge!"

"We should call my mother!"

"We should look for clues!"

"We should look for weapons!"

"We should look for my mother!"

"We should look for suspicious people!"

"Suspicious people?" repeated another voice. "But this is supposed to be a nice hotel!"

"Nice hotels are crawling with suspicious people," someone else remarked. "I saw a wash-erwoman who was wearing a suspicious wig!"

"I saw a concierge carrying a suspicious item!"

"I saw a taxi carrying a suspicious passenger!"

"I saw a cook preparing suspicious food!"

"I saw an attendant holding a suspicious spatula!"

"I saw a man with a suspicious cloud of smoke!"

"I saw a baby with a suspicious lock!"

"I saw a manager wearing a suspicious uniform!"

"I saw a woman wearing suspicious lettuce!"

"I saw my mother!"

"I can't see anything!" someone yelled. "It's as dark as a crow flying through a pitch black night!"

"I see something right now!" cried a voice. "There are three suspicious people standing at the edge of the pond!"

"They're the people who were talking to the reporter!" cried somebody else. "They're refusing to show their faces!"

"They must be murderers!" cried yet another person. "Nobody else would act as suspiciously as that!"

"We'd better hurry downstairs," said one more guest, "before they escape!"

"Wow!" squealed another voice. "Wait until the readers of *The Daily Punctilio* read the headline: 'VICIOUS MURDER AT HOTEL DENOUEMENT!'

That's much more exciting than an accident!"

"Mob psychology," Sunny said, remembering a term Klaus had taught her shortly before she took her first steps.

"Sunny's right," said Klaus, wiping his eyes. "This crowd is getting angrier and angrier. In a moment, they'll all believe we're murderers."

"Maybe we are," Violet said quietly.

"Poppycock!" Sunny said firmly, which meant something like, "Nonsense." "Accident!"

"It was an accident," Klaus said, "but it was our fault."

"Partially," Sunny said.

"It's not for us to decide," Violet said. "We should go inside and talk to Justice Strauss and the others. They'll know what to do."

"Maybe," Klaus said. "Or maybe we should run."

"Run?" Sunny asked.

"We can't run," Violet said. "If we run, everyone will think we're murderers."

"Maybe we are," Klaus pointed out. "All the noble people in that lobby have failed us. We can't be sure they'll help us now."

Violet heaved a great sigh, her breath still shaky from her tears. "Where would we go?" she whispered.

"Anywhere," Klaus said simply. "We could go somewhere where no one has ever heard of Count Olaf, or V.F.D. There must be other noble people in the world, and we could find them."

"There are other noble people," Violet said. "They're on their way here. Dewey told us to wait until tomorrow. I think we should stay."

"Tomorrow might be too late," Klaus said. "I think we should run."

"Torn," Sunny said, which meant something along the lines of, "I see the advantages and disadvantages of both plans of action," but before her siblings could answer, the children felt a shadow over them, and looked up to see a tall, skinny figure standing over them. In the darkness the children could not see any of his features, only the glowing tip of a skinny cigarette in his mouth.

"Do you three need a taxi?" he asked, and gestured to the automobile that had brought Justice Strauss and Jerome Squalor to the entrance of the hotel.

The siblings looked at one another, and then squinted up at the man. The children thought perhaps his voice was familiar, but it might just have been his unfathomable tone, which they'd heard so many times since their arrival at the hotel that it made everything seem familiar and mysterious at the same time.

"We're not sure," Violet said, after a moment.

"You're not sure?" the man asked. "Whenever you see someone in a taxi, they are probably being driven to do some errand. Surely there must be something you need to do, or somewhere you need to go. A great American novelist wrote that people travel faster now, but she wasn't sure if they do better things. Maybe you would do better things if you traveled at this very moment."

"We haven't any money," Klaus said.

"You needn't worry about money," the man said, "not if you're who I think you are." He leaned in toward the Baudelaires. "Are you?" he asked. "Are you who I think you are?"

The children looked at each other again. They had no way of knowing, of course, if this man was a volunteer or an enemy, a noble man or a treacherous person. In general, of course, a stranger who tries to get you into an automobile is anything but noble, and in general a person who quotes great American novelists is anything but treacherous, and in general a man who says you needn't worry about money, or a man who smokes cigarettes, is somewhere in between. But the Baudelaire orphans were not standing in general. They were standing outside the Hotel Denouement, at the edge of a pond where a great secret was hidden, while a crowd

of guests grew more and more suspicious about
the terrible thing that had just occurred. The
children thought of Dewey, and remembered
the terrible, terrible sight of him sinking into
the pond, and they realized they had no way of
knowing if they themselves were good or evil,
let alone the mysterious man towering over
them.

"We don't know," Sunny said finally.

"Baudelaires!" came a sharp voice at the top
of the stairs, followed by a fit of coughing, and
the siblings turned to see Mr. Poe, who was staring at the children and covering his mouth with
a white handkerchief. "What has happened?"
he asked. "Where is that man you shot with the
harpoon?"

The Baudelaires were too weary and
unhappy to argue with Mr. Poe's description of
what happened. "He's dead," Violet said, and
found that tears were in her eyes once more.

Mr. Poe coughed once more in astonishment, and then stepped down the stairs and

stood in front of the children whose welfare had been his responsibility. "Dead!" he said. "How did that happen?"

"It's difficult to say," Klaus said.

"Difficult to say?" Mr. Poe frowned. "But I saw you, Baudelaires. You were holding the weapon. Surely you can tell me what happened."

"Henribergson," Sunny said, which meant "It's more complicated than that," but Mr. Poe only shook his head as if he'd heard enough.

"You'd better come inside," he said, with a weary sigh. "I must say I'm very disappointed in you children. When I was in charge of your affairs, no matter how many homes I found for you, terrible things occurred. Then, when you decided to handle your own affairs, *The Daily Punctilio* brought more and more news of your treachery with each passing day. And now that I've found you again, I see that once more an unfortunate event has occurred, and another guardian is dead. You should be ashamed of yourselves."

The Baudelaires did not answer. Dewey Denouement, of course, had not been their official guardian at the Hotel Denouement, but he had looked after them, even when they did not know it, and he had done his best to protect them from the villainous people lurking around their home. Even though he wasn't a proper guardian, he was a good guardian, and the children were ashamed of themselves for their participation in his unfortunate death. In silence, they waited while Mr. Poe had another fit of coughing, and then the banker put his hands on the Baudelaires' shoulders, pushing them toward the entrance to the hotel. "There are people who say that criminal behavior is the destiny of children from a broken home," he said. "Perhaps such people are right."

"This isn't our destiny," Klaus said, but he did not sound very sure, and Mr. Poe merely gave him a sad, stern look, and kept pushing. If someone taller than you has ever reached down to push you by the shoulder, then you know this is not a pleasant way to travel, but the Baudelaires were too upset and confused to care. Up the stairs they went, the banker plodding behind them in his ugly pajamas, and only when they reached the cloud of steam that still wafted across the entrance did they think to look back at the mysterious man who had offered them a ride. By then the man was already back inside the taxi and was driving slowly away from the Hotel Denouement, and just as the children had no way of knowing if he was a good person or not, they had no way of knowing if they were sad or relieved to see him go, and even after months of research, and many sleepless nights, and many dreary afternoons spent in front of an enormous pond, throwing stones in the hopes that someone would notice the ripples I was making, I have no way of knowing if the Baude- laires should have been sad or relieved to see

him go either. I do know who the man was, and
I do know where he went afterward, and I do
know the name of the woman who was hiding
in the trunk, and the type of musical instrument
that was laid carefully in the back seat, and the
ingredients of the sandwich tucked into the
glove compartment, and even the small item
that sat on the passenger seat, still damp from
its hiding place, but I cannot tell you if the
Baudelaires would have been happier in this
man's company, or if it was better that he drove
away from the three siblings, looking back at
them through the rearview mirror and clutching
a monogrammed napkin in his trembling hand.
I do know that if they had gotten into his taxi,
their troubles at the Hotel Denouement would
not have been their penultimate peril, and they
would have had quite a few more woeful events
in their lives that would likely take thirteen
more books to describe, but I have no way of
knowing if it would have been better for the
orphans, any more than I know if it would have

been better for me had I decided to continue my life's work rather than researching the Baudelaires' story, or if it would have been better for my sister had she decided to join the children at the Hotel Denouement instead of waterskiing toward Captain Widdershins, and, later, waterskiing away from him, or if it would have been better for you to step into that taxi-cab you saw not so long ago and embark on your own series of events, rather than continuing with the life you have for yourself. There is no way of knowing. When there is no way of knowing, one can only imagine, and I imagine that the Baudelaire orphans were quite frightened indeed when they walked through the entrance to the hotel and saw the crowd of people waiting for them in the lobby.

"There they are!" roared someone from the back of the room. The children could not see who it was, because the lobby was as crowded as it had been when they first set foot in the perplexing hotel. It had been strange to walk through the enormous, domed room that morning, passing unnoticed in their concierge disguises, but this time every person in the lobby was looking directly at them. The children were amazed to see countless familiar faces from every chapter of their lives, and saw many, many people they could not be sure if they recognized or not. Everyone was wearing pajamas, nightgowns, or other sleepwear, and was glaring at the Baudelaires through eyes squinty from being awakened in the middle of the night. It is always interesting to observe what people are wearing in the middle of the night, although there are more pleasant ways to make such observations without being accused of murder. "Those are the murderers!"

"They're no ordinary murderers!" cried Geraldine Julienne, who was wearing a bright yellow nightshirt and had a shower cap over her hair. "They're the Baudelaire orphans!"

A ripple of astonishment went through the pajamaed crowd, and the children wished they had thought to put their sunglasses back on. "The Baudelaire orphans?" cried Sir, whose pajamas had the initials L. S. stenciled over the pocket, presumably for "Lucky Smells." "I remember them! They caused accidents in my lumbermill!"

"The accidents weren't their fault!" Charles said, whose pajamas matched his partner's. "They were the fault of Count Olaf!"

"Count Olaf is another one of their victims!" cried a woman dressed in a bright pink bathrobe. The Baudelaires recognized her as Mrs. Morrow, one of the citizens of the Village of Fowl Devotees. "He was murdered right in my hometown!"

"That was Count Omar," said another citizen of the town, a man named Mr. Lesko who apparently slept in the same plaid pants he wore during the day.

"I'm sure the Baudelaires aren't murderers," said Jerome Squalor. "I was their guardian, and I always found them to be polite and kind."

"They were pretty good students, if I remember correctly," said Mr. Remora, who was wearing a nightcap shaped like a banana.

"They were pretty good students, if I remember correctly," Vice Principal Nero mimicked. "They were nothing of the sort. Violet and Klaus flunked all sorts of tests, and Sunny was the worst administrative assistant I've ever seen!"

"I say they're criminals," Mrs. Bass said, adjusting her wig, "and criminals ought to be punished."

"Yes!" said Hugo. "Criminals are too freakish to be running around loose!"

"They're not criminals," Hal said firmly, "and I should know."

"So should I," retorted Esmé Squalor, "and I say they're guilty as sin." Her long, silver fingernails rested on the shoulder of Carmelita Spats, who was glaring at the siblings as Mr. Poe pushed them past.

"I think they're guiltier than that!" said one of the hotel bellboys.

"I think they're even guiltier than you think they are!" cried another.

"I think they look like nice kids!" said someone the children did not recognize.

"I think they look like vicious criminals!" said another person.

"I think they look like noble volunteers!" said another.

"I think they look like treacherous villains!"

"I think they look like concierges!"

"One of them looks a bit like my mother!"

Wrong! Wrong! Wrong! The lobby seemed to shake as the clock struck three in the morning. By now, Mr. Poe had escorted the Baudelaires to a far corner of the lobby, where either Frank or Ernest was waiting next to the door marked 121 with a grim expression on his face as the last *Wrong!* echoed in the enormous room.

"Ladies and gentlemen!" The children turned to see Justice Strauss, who was standing on one of the wooden benches so she could be seen and clapping her hands for attention.

"Please settle down! The matter of the Baude-laires' guilt or innocence is not for you to decide."

"That doesn't seem fair," remarked a man in pajamas with a pattern of salmon swimming upstream. "After all, they woke us up in the middle of the night."

"The case is a matter for the High Court," Justice Strauss said. "The authorities have been notified, and the other judges of the court are on their way. We will be able to begin the trial in a matter of hours."

"I thought the trial was on Thursday," said a woman in a nightgown emblazoned with danc-ing clowns.

"Showing up early is one of the signs of a noble person," Justice Strauss said. "Once the other noble judges have arrived, we will decide on this matter—and other equally important matters—once and for all."

There was a murmur of discussion in the crowd. "I suppose that's all right," grumbled someone.

"All right?" Geraldine Julienne said. "It's wonderful! I can see the headline now: 'HIGH COURT FINDS BAUDELAIRES GUILTY!'"

"No one is guilty until the trial is over," Justice Strauss said, and for the first time the judge gazed down at the children and gave them a gentle smile. It was a small mercy, that smile, and the frightened Baudelaires smiled back. Justice Strauss stepped off the bench and walked through the murmuring crowd, followed by Jerome Squalor.

"Don't worry, children," Jerome said. "It looks like you won't have to wait until tomorrow for justice to be served."

"I hope so," Violet said.

"I thought judges weren't allowed to reach verdicts on people they know," Klaus said.

"Normally that's true," Justice Strauss said. "The law should be impartial and fair. But I think I can be fair where Count Olaf is concerned."

"Besides," Jerome said, "there are two other

judges on the High Court. Justice Strauss's opinion is not the only one that matters."

"I trust my fellow judges," Justice Strauss said. "I've known them for years, and they've always been concerned whenever I've reported on your case. While we wait for them to arrive, however, I've asked the managers of the hotel to put you in Room 121, to keep you away from this angry crowd."

Without a word, Frank or Ernest unlocked the door and revealed the small, bare closet where Violet had found the harpoon gun. "We'll be locked up?" Klaus said nervously.

"Just to keep you safe," Justice Strauss said, "until the trial begins."

"Yes!" cried a voice the children would never forget. The crowd parted to reveal Count Olaf, who walked toward the Baudelaires with a triumphant gleam in his eyes. "Lock them up!" he said. "We can't have treacherous people running around the hotel! There are noble, decent people here."

"Really?" asked Colette.

"Ha!" Count Olaf said. "I mean, of course! The High Court will decide who's noble and who's wicked. In the meantime, the orphans should be locked in a closet."

"Hear hear!" Kevin said, raising one arm and then the other in an ambidextrous salute.

"They're not the only ones," Justice Strauss said sternly. "You, sir, have also been accused of a great deal of treachery, and the High Court is very interested in your case as well. You will be locked in Room 165 until the trial begins."

The man who was not Frank but Ernest, or vice versa, stepped sternly out of the crowd and took Olaf's arm.

"Fair enough," said Olaf. "I'm happy to wait for the verdict of the High Court. Ha!"

The three siblings looked at one another, and then around the lobby, where the crowd was looking fiercely back at them. They did not want to be locked in a small room, no matter what the reason, and they could not understand why the idea of the High Court reaching a verdict on Count Olaf made him laugh. However, they knew that arguing with the crowd would be bootless, a word which here means "likely to get the siblings in even more trouble," and so without another word, the three Baudelaires stepped inside the closet. Jerome and Justice Strauss gave them a little wave, and Mr. Poe gave them a little cough, and either Frank or Ernest stepped forward to shut the door. At the sight of the manager, the children suddenly thought not of Dewey, but of the family left behind, just as Violet, Klaus, and Sunny were all left behind after that first day at Briny Beach, and the dreadful news they received there.

"We're sorry," Sunny said, and the manager looked down at the youngest Baudelaire and blinked. Perhaps he was Frank, and thought the Baudelaires had done something wicked, or perhaps he was Ernest, and thought the Baudelaires had done something noble, but in either case the manager looked surprised that the children were sorry. For a moment, he paused, and gave them a tiny nod, but then he shut the door and the Baudelaire children were alone. The door of Room 121 was surprisingly thick, and although the light of the lobby shone clearly through the gap at the bottom of the door, the noise of the crowd was nothing but a faint buzzing, like a swarm of bees or the workings of a machine. The orphans sank to the floor, exhausted from their busy day and their terrible, terrible night. They took off their shoes and leaned against one another in the cramped surroundings, trying to find a comfortable position and listening to the buzz of the arguing crowd in the lobby.

"What will happen to us?" Violet asked.

"I don't know," Klaus said.

"Perhaps we should have run," Violet said, "like you suggested, Klaus."

"Perhaps at a trial," the middle Baudelaire said, "the villains at last will be brought to justice."

"Olaf," Sunny asked, "or us?"

What Sunny asked, of course, was whether Count Olaf was the villain who would be brought to justice, or if it would be the three Baudelaires, but her siblings had no answer for her. Instead, the eldest Baudelaire leaned down and kissed the top of her sister's head, and Klaus leaned up to kiss Violet's, and Sunny moved her head first to the right and then to the left, to kiss both of them. If you had been in the lobby of the Hotel Denouement, you would not have heard anything from behind the thick door of Room 121, as the Baudelaires ended their conversation with a great, shuddering sigh, and nestled close to one another in the small space. You would have had to be on the other side of the door, leaning against the children yourself, to hear the tiny, quiet sounds as the Baudelaire orphans cried themselves to sleep, unable to answer Sunny's question.

Eleven

An old expression, used even before the schism, says that people should not see the creation of laws or sausages. This makes sense, as the creation of sausages involves taking various parts of different animals and shaping them until they are presentable at breakfast, and the creation of laws involves taking various parts of different ideas and shaping them until they are presentable at breakfast, and most people prefer to spend their breakfasts eating food and reading the newspaper without being exposed to creation of any sort whatsoever.

The High Court, like most courts, was not

involved in the creation of laws, but it was involved in the interpretation of laws, which is as perplexing and unfathomable as their creation, and like the interpretation of sausages is something that also should not be seen. If you were to put this book down, and travel to the pond that now reflects nothing but a few burnt scraps of wood and the empty skies, and if you were to find the hidden passageway that leads to the underwater catalog that has remained secret and safe for all these years, you could read an account of an interpretation of sausages that went horribly wrong and led to the destruction of a very important bathyscaphe, all because I mistakenly thought the sausages were arranged in the shape of a K when actually the waiter had been trying to make an R, and an account of an interpretation of the law that went horribly wrong, although it would hardly be worth the trip as that account is also contained in the remaining chapters of this book, but if you were at all sensible you would shield your eyes from such interpretations, as they are too dreadful to read. As Violet, Klaus, and Sunny caught a few winks—a phrase which here means "slept fitfully in the closet-sized Room 121"—arrangements were made for the trial, during which the three judges of the High Court would interpret the laws and decide on the nobility and treachery of Count Olaf and the Baudelaires, but the children were surprised to learn, when a sharp knock on the door awakened them, that they would not see this interpretation themselves.

"Here are your blindfolds," said one of the managers, opening the door and handing the children three pieces of black cloth. The Baudelaires suspected he was Ernest, as he hadn't bothered to say "Hello."

"Blindfolds?" Violet asked.

"Everyone wears blindfolds at a High Court trial," the manager replied, "except the judges, of course. Haven't you heard the expression 'Justice is blind'?"

"Yes," Klaus said, "but I always thought it

meant that justice should be fair and unprejudiced."

"The verdict of the High Court was to take the expression literally," said the manager, "so everyone except the judges must cover their eyes before the trial can begin."

"Scalia," Sunny said. She meant something like, "It doesn't seem like the literal interpretation makes any sense," but her siblings did not think it was wise to translate.

"I also brought you some tea," he said, revealing a tray containing a teapot and three cups. "I thought it might fortify you for the trial."

By "fortify," the manager meant that a few sips of tea might give the children some much-needed strength for their ordeal, and the children thought it must be Frank who was doing them such a favor. "You're very kind," Violet said.

"I'm sorry there's no sugar," he said.

"That's quite all right," Klaus said, and then hurriedly flipped to a page in his commonplace book until he found his notes on the children's conversation with Kit Snicket. "'Tea should be bitter as wormwood,'" he read, "'and as sharp as a two-edged sword.'"

The manager gave Klaus a small, unfathomable smile. "Drink your tea," he said. "I'll knock in a few minutes to bring you to trial."

Frank, unless it was Ernest, shut the door, and left the Baudelaires alone.

"Why did you say that about the tea?" Violet asked.

"I thought he might be talking to us in code," Klaus said. "I thought if we gave the proper reply, something might happen."

"Unfathomable," Sunny said.

"Everything seems unfathomable," Violet said with a sigh, pouring tea for her siblings. "It's getting so that I can't tell a noble person from a wicked one."

"Kit said that the only way to tell a villain from a volunteer is to observe everyone, and make such judgements ourselves," Klaus said, "but that hasn't helped us at all."

"Today the High Court will do the judging for us," Violet said. "Maybe they'll prove to be helpful."

"Or fail us," Sunny said.

The eldest Baudelaire smiled, and reached to help her sister put on her shoes. "I wish our parents could see how much you've grown," she said. "Mother always said that as soon as you learned to walk, Sunny, you'd be going places."

"I doubt a closet in the Hotel Denouement was what she had in mind," Klaus said, blowing on his tea to cool it.

"Who knows what they had in mind?" Violet asked. "That's one more mystery we'll probably never solve."

Sunny took a sip of tea, which was indeed as bitter as wormwood and as sharp as a two-edged sword, although the youngest Baudelaire had little experience with metallic weapons or hoary aromatic plants of the composite family, used in certain recreational tonics. "Mama and Poppa," she said hesitantly, "and poison darts?"

Her siblings did not have time to answer, as there was another knock on the door. "Finish your tea," called either Frank or Ernest, "and put on your blindfolds. The trial is about to begin."

The Baudelaires hurried to follow the instructions of either the volunteer or the villain, and took a few quick sips of their tea, tied their shoes, and wound the pieces of cloth around their eyes. In a moment they heard the door of Room 121 open, and heard Frank or Ernest step toward them.

"Where are you?" he asked.

"We're right here," Violet said. "Can't you see us?"

"Of course not," the manager replied. "I'm also wearing a blindfold. Reach for my hand, and I'll lead you to the trial."

The eldest Baudelaire reached out in front of her and found a large, rough hand awaiting hers. Klaus took Violet's other hand, and Sunny took Klaus's, and in this way the children were

led out of Room 121. The expression "the blind
leading the blind," like the expression "Justice
is blind," is usually not taken literally, as it
simply refers to a confusing situation in which
the people in charge know nothing more than
the people following them. But as the Baudelaires learned as they were led through the
lobby, the blindfolded leading the blindfolded
results in the same sort of confusion. The children could not see anything through their blindfolds, but the room was filled with the sounds
of people looking for their companions, bumping up against one another, and running into the
walls and furniture. Violet was poked in the eye
by someone's chubby finger. Klaus was mistaken for someone named Jerry by a man who
gave him an enormous hug before learning of
his mistake. And someone bumped into Sunny's
head, assumed she was an ornamental vase, and
tried to place an umbrella in her mouth. Above
the noise of the crowd, the Baudelaires heard
the clock strike twelve insistent *Wrong!*s, and

realized they had been sleeping quite some time. It was already Wednesday afternoon, which meant that Thursday, and the arrival of their noble friends and associates, was quite close indeed.

"Attention!" The voice of Justice Strauss was also quite close indeed, and rang out over the crowd, along with the repeated banging of a gavel, a word which refers to the small hammer used by judges when they want someone's attention. "Attention everyone! The trial is about to begin! Everyone please take your seats!"

"How can we take our seats," a man asked, "when we can't see them?"

"Feel around with your hands," Justice Strauss said. "Move to your right. Further. Further. Further. Furth—"

"Ow!"

"Not that far," the judge said. "There! Sit! Now the rest of you follow his lead!"

"How can we do what he did," asked someone else, "if we can't see him?"

"Can we peek?" asked another person.

"No peeking!" Justice Strauss said sternly. "Our system of justice isn't perfect, but it's the only one we have. I remind you that all three judges of the High Court are bare-eyed, and if you peek you will be guilty of contempt of court! 'Contempt,' by the way, is a word for finding something worthless or dishonorable."

"I know what the word 'contempt' means," snarled a voice the children could not recognize.

"I defined the word for the benefit of the Baudelaires," Justice Strauss said, and the children nodded their thanks in the direction of the judge's voice, although all three siblings had known the meaning of "contempt" since a night long ago when Uncle Monty had taken them to the movies. "Baudelaires, take three steps to your right. Three more. One more. There! You've reached your bench. Please sit down."

The Baudelaires sat down on one of the lobby's wooden benches and listened to the footsteps of the manager as he left them alone and stumbled back into the settling crowd. Finally, it sounded as if everyone had found a seat of some kind or another, and with another few bangs of the gavel and calls for attention, the crowd quieted down and Justice Strauss began the trial.

"Good afternoon, ladies and gentlemen," she said, her voice coming from right in front of the Baudelaires, "and anyone else who happens to be in attendance. It has come to the attention of the High Court that certain wicked deeds have gone unpunished, and that this wickedness is continuing at an alarming rate. We planned to hold a trial on Thursday, but after the death of Mr. Denouement it is clear we should proceed earlier, in the interests of justice and nobility. We will hear what each witness has to say and determine once and for all who is responsible. The guilty parties will be turned over to the authorities, who are waiting outside, making sure that no one will try to escape while the trial is in progress."

"And speaking of guilty parties," Count Olaf added, "when the trial is over, everyone is invited to a very in cocktail party, hosted by me! Wealthy women are particularly welcome!"

"I'm hosting it," snarled the voice of Esmé Squalor, "and fashionable men will be given a free gift."

"All gifts are free," said either Frank or Ernest.

"You're out of order," Justice Strauss said sternly, banging her gavel. "We are discussing social justice, not social engagements. Now then, will the accused parties please stand and state their names and occupations for the record?"

The Baudelaires stood up hesitantly.

"You too, Count Olaf," Justice Strauss said firmly. The wooden bench crackled beside the Baudelaires, and they realized the notorious villain had also been sitting on the bench, and was now standing beside them.

"Name?" the judge asked.

"Count Olaf," Count Olaf replied.

"Occupation?"

"Impresario," he said, using a fancy word for someone who puts on theatrical spectacles.

"And are you innocent or guilty?" asked Justice Strauss.

The children thought they could hear Olaf's filthy teeth slide against his lips as he smiled. "I'm unspeakably innocent," he said, and murmuring spread through the crowd like a ripple on the surface of a pond.

"You may be seated," Justice Strauss said, banging her gavel. "Children, you are next. Please state your names."

"Violet Baudelaire," said Violet Baudelaire.

"Klaus Baudelaire," said Klaus Baudelaire.

"Sunny Baudelaire," said Sunny Baudelaire.

The children heard the scratching of a pen, and realized that the judge was writing down everything that was being said. "Occupations?"

The Baudelaires did not know how to answer this question. The word "occupation," as I'm sure you know, usually refers to a job, but the Baudelaires' employment was sporadic, a word which here means "consisting of a great number of occupations, held for a short time and under very unusual circumstances." The word can also refer to how one spends one's time, but the siblings hardly liked to think of all the dreadful things that had occupied them recently. Lastly, the word "occupation" can refer to the state one is in, such as being a woman's husband, or a child's guardian, but the young-sters were not certain how such a term could apply to the bewildering history of their lives. The Baudelaires thought and thought, and finally each gave their answer as they saw fit.

"Volunteer," Violet said.

"Concierge," Klaus said.

"Child," Sunny said.

"I object!" Olaf said beside them. "Their proper occupation is orphan, or inheritor of a large fortune!"

"Your objection is noted," Justice Strauss

said firmly. "Now then, Baudelaires, are you guilty or innocent?"

Once again, the Baudelaires hesitated before answering. Justice Strauss had not asked the children precisely what they were innocent or guilty of, and the expectant hush of the lobby did not make them want to ask the judge to clarify her question. In general, of course, the Baudelaire children believed themselves to be innocent, although they were certainly guilty, as we all are, of certain deeds that are anything but noble. But the Baudelaires were not standing in general. They were standing next to Count Olaf. It was Klaus who found the words to compare the siblings' innocence and guilt with the innocence and guilt of a man who said he was unspeakably innocent, and after a pause the middle Baudelaire answered the judge's question.

"We're comparatively innocent," he said, and a ripple went through the crowd again. The children heard the scratching of Justice Strauss's

pen again, and the sound of Geraldine Julienne's enthusiastic voice.

"I can see the headlines now!" she cried.
"'EVERYBODY IS INNOCENT!' Wait until the readers of *The Daily Punctilio* see that!"

"Nobody is innocent," Justice Strauss said,
banging her gavel. "At least, not yet. Now then,
all those in the courtroom who have evidence
they would like to submit to the court, please
approach the judges and do so."

The room erupted into pandemonium, a word
which here means "a crowd of blindfolded people
attempting to give evidence to three judges."
The Baudelaires sat on the bench and heard
people stumbling over one another as they all
tried to submit their research to the High Court.

"I submit these newspaper articles!" announced the voice of Geraldine Julienne.

"I submit these employment records!"
announced Sir.

"I submit these environmental studies!"
announced Charles.

"I submit these grade books!" announced Mr. Remora.

"I submit these blueprints of banks!" announced Mrs. Bass.

"I submit these administrative records!" announced Vice Principal Nero.

"I submit this paperwork!" announced Hal.

"I submit these financial records!" announced Mr. Poe.

"I submit these rule books!" announced Mr. Lesko.

"I submit these constitutions!" announced Mrs. Morrow.

"I submit these carnival posters!" announced Hugo.

"I submit these anatomical drawings!" announced Colette.

"I submit these books," announced Kevin, "with both my left and right hands!"

"I submit these ruby-encrusted blank pages!" announced Esmé Squalor.

"I submit this book about how wonderful

I am!" announced Carmelita Spats.

"I submit this commonplace book!" announced either Frank or Ernest.

"So do I!" announced either Ernest or Frank.

"I submit my mother!"

This last voice was the first in a parade of voices the Baudelaires could not recognize. It seemed that everyone in the lobby had something to submit to the High Court, and the Baudelaires felt as if they were in the middle of an avalanche of observations, research, and other evidence, some of which sounded exculpatory—a word which here means "likely to prove that the Baudelaires were innocent"— and some of which sounded damning, a word which made the children shudder just to think of it.

"I submit these photographs!"

"I submit these hospital records!"

"I submit these magazine articles!"

"I submit these telegrams!"

"I submit these couplets!"

"I submit these maps!"

"I submit these cookbooks!"

"I submit these scraps of paper!"

"I submit these screenplays!"

"I submit these rhyming dictionaries!"

"I submit these love letters!"

"I submit these opera synopses!"

"I submit these thesauri!"

"I submit these marriage licenses!"

"I submit these Talmudic commentaries!"

"I submit these wills and testaments!"

"I submit these auction catalogs!"

"I submit these codebooks!"

"I submit these mycological encyclopedias!"

"I submit these menus!"

"I submit these ferry schedules!"

"I submit these theatrical programs!"

"I submit these business cards!"

"I submit these memos!"

"I submit these novels!"

"I submit these cookies!"

"I submit these assorted pieces of evidence I'm unwilling to categorize!"

Finally, the Baudelaires heard a mighty *thump!* and the triumphant voice of Jerome Squalor. "I submit this comprehensive history of injustice!" he announced, and the lobby filled with the sound of applause and of hissing, as the volunteers and villains reacted. Justice Strauss had to bang her gavel quite a few times before the crowd settled down.

"Before the High Court reviews this evidence," the judge said, "we ask each accused person to give a statement explaining their actions. You can take as long as you want to tell your story, but you should leave out nothing important. Count Olaf, you may go first."

The wooden bench crackled again as the villain stood up, and the Baudelaires heard Count Olaf sigh, and smelled his foul breath. "Ladies and gentlemen," he said, "I'm so incredibly innocent that the word 'innocent' ought to be written on my face in capital letters. The letter I would stand for 'I'm innocent.' The letter N would stand for 'nothing wrong,' which is what I've done. The letter A would stand for—"

"That's not how you spell 'innocent,'" Justice Strauss interrupted.

"I don't think spelling counts," Count Olaf grumbled.

"Spelling counts," the judge said sternly.

"Well, 'innocence' should be spelled O-L-A-F," Count Olaf said, "and that's the end of my speech."

The bench crackled as Olaf sat down.

"That's all you have to say?" Justice Strauss asked in surprise.

"Yep," Count Olaf said.

"I told you not to leave out anything important," the judge reminded him.

"I'm the only important thing," Count Olaf insisted, "and I'm very innocent. I'm sure there's more in that enormous pile of evidence that proves me innocent than there is that proves me guilty."

"Well, all right," the judge said uncertainly. "Baudelaires, you may now tell us your side of the story."

The Baudelaires stood up unsteadily, their legs trembling in nervous anticipation, but once again they did not quite know what to say.

"Go on," Justice Strauss said kindly. "We're listening."

The Baudelaire orphans clasped hands. Although they had just been notified about the trial a few hours ago, the children felt as if they had been waiting forever to stand and tell their story to anyone who might listen. Although much of their story had been told to Mr. Poe, and noted in Klaus's commonplace book, and discussed with the Quagmire triplets and other noble people they had met during their travels, they had never had the opportunity to tell their entire tale, from the dreadful day at Briny Beach when Mr. Poe gave them the terrible news about their parents, to this very afternoon, as they stood at the High Court hoping that all of the villains in their lives would at last be brought to justice. Perhaps there had never been enough time to sit and tell their story just as they wanted to tell it, or perhaps their story was so unhappy that they dared not share all of the wretched details with anyone. Or perhaps the Baudelaires had simply not encountered anyone who listened to them as well as their parents had. As the siblings stood before the High Court, they could picture the faces of their mother and father, and the expressions they wore when listening to their children. Occasionally, one of the Baudelaires would be telling their parents a story, and there would be an interruption of some kind—the ringing of the phone, or the loud noise of a siren outside, or even a remark from one of the other siblings. "Hush," the Baudelaire parents would say to the interruption. "It's not your day in court," they would say, and then they would turn back to the Baudelaire who was talking, and give them a nod to indicate that the story should continue. The children stood together, as the wooden bench creaked behind them, and started to tell the story of their lives, a story they had waited their lives to tell.

"Well," Violet said, "one afternoon my siblings and I were at Briny Beach. I was dreaming up an invention that could retrieve a rock after you skipped it into the ocean. Klaus was examining creatures in tidepools. And Sunny noticed that Mr. Poe was walking toward us."

"Hmm," Justice Strauss said, but it wasn't a thoughtful kind of "hmm." Violet thought perhaps that the judge was saying "hmm" the way she had said "hmm" to either Frank or Ernest, as a safe answer.

"Go on," said a low, deep voice that belonged to one of the other judges. "Justice Strauss was merely being thoughtful."

"Mr. Poe told us that there had been a

terrible fire," Klaus continued. "Our home was destroyed, and our parents were gone."

"Hmm," Justice Strauss said again, but it wasn't a sympathetic kind of "hmm." Klaus thought perhaps that the judge was taking a sip of tea, to fortify herself as the siblings told their story.

"Please continue," said another voice. This one was very hoarse, as if the third judge had been screaming for hours and could hardly talk. "Justice Strauss was merely being sympathetic."

"Bildungsroman," said Sunny. She meant something along the lines of, "Since that moment, our story has been a long, dreadful education in the wicked ways of the world and the mysterious secrets hidden in all of its corners," but before her siblings could translate, Justice Strauss uttered another "hmm," and this one was the strangest of all. It was not a thoughtful "hmm," nor did it sound like a safe answer, and it certainly wasn't sympathetic, or the noise someone might make while taking a sip of tea. To Sunny the "hmm" sounded like a noise she'd heard a long time ago, not long after the day on Briny Beach the children were describing. The youngest Baudelaire had heard the same noise coming from her own mouth, when she was dangling outside Count Olaf's tower room in a bird cage with a piece of tape covering her mouth. Sunny gasped, recognizing the sound just as Klaus recognized the voice of the second judge, and Violet recognized the voice of the third. Blindly, the Baudelaires reached out their hands to clutch one another in panic.

"What shall we do?" Violet whispered, as quietly as possible.

"Peek," Sunny whispered back.

"If we peek," Klaus whispered, "we'll be guilty of contempt of court."

"What are you waiting for, orphans?" asked the low, deep voice.

"Yes," said the hoarse one. "Continue your story."

But the Baudelaire orphans knew they could not continue their story, no matter how long they had been waiting to tell it. At the sound of those familiar voices, they had no choice but to remove their blindfolds. The children did not care if they were guilty of contempt of court, because they knew that if the other two judges were who they thought they were, then the High Court was indeed something they found worthless or dishonorable, and so without any further discussion they unwound the pieces of black cloth that covered their eyes, and the Baudelaire orphans peeked.

It was a shocking and upsetting peek that awaited the Baudelaires. Squinting in the sudden light, they peeked straight ahead, where the voices of Justice Strauss and the other judges had come from. The children found themselves peeking at the concierge desk, which was piled with all the evidence the crowd had submitted, including newspaper articles, employment records, environmental studies, grade books, blueprints of banks, administrative records, paperwork, financial records, rule books, constitutions, carnival posters, anatomical drawings, books, ruby-encrusted blank pages, a book alleging how wonderful Carmelita Spats was, commonplace books, photographs, hospital records, magazine articles, telegrams, couplets, maps, cookbooks, scraps of paper, screenplays, rhyming dictionaries, love letters, opera synopses, thesauri, marriage licenses, Talmudic commentaries, wills and testaments, auction catalogs, codebooks, mycological encyclopedias, menus, ferry schedules, theatrical programs, business cards, memos, novels, cookies, assorted pieces of evidence a certain person was unwilling to categorize, and someone's mother, all of which Dewey Denouement had been hoping to catalog. Missing from the desk, however, was Justice Strauss, and as the Baudelaires peeked around the lobby, they saw that another person was missing, too, for there was no one on the wooden bench, only a few etched rings from people wicked enough to set down glasses without using coasters. Frantically, they peeked through the blindfolded crowd that was waiting impatiently for them to continue their story, and finally they spotted Count Olaf at the far side of the room. Justice Strauss was there, too, tucked in the crook of Olaf's arm the way you might carry an umbrella if both your hands were full. Neither of Count Olaf's filthy hands were full, but they were both otherwise engaged, a phrase which here means that one hand was covering Justice Strauss's mouth with tape, so she could only say "hmm," and the other was hurriedly pressing the button requesting an elevator. The harpoon gun, with its last hook gleaming wickedly, was leaning against the wall, within easy reach of the treacherous villain.

All this was a shocking and upsetting peek, of course, but even more shocking and upsetting was what the children saw when they returned their gaze to the concierge desk. For sitting at either end, with their elbows on the pile of evidence, were two villains at whom the children had hoped very much they would never get a peek again, villains of such wickedness that it is far too shocking and upsetting for me to write down their names. I can only describe them as the man with a beard, but no hair, and the woman with hair, but no beard, but to the Baudelaire orphans, these two villainous judges were another peek at the wicked way of the world.

CHAPTER Twelve

The man with a beard but no hair stood up from
the concierge desk, his knees bumping against
the little bells that had sent the Baudelaire
orphans on their errands. The woman with hair
but no beard pointed a finger at the three children that looked as crooked as she was. The finger had been broken long ago, in a dispute over

a game of backgammon, which is another story that would take at least thirteen books to describe, but in the Baudelaires' story the finger only made this brief appearance as it pointed at the children in alarm.

"The Baudelaires have taken off their blindfolds!" cried the villainous woman in her low, deep voice.

"Yes!" agreed the villainous man, in his hoarse voice. "They're guilty of contempt of court!"

"We certainly are," Violet agreed fiercely. "This court is worthless and dishonorable!"

"Two of the judges are notorious villains," Klaus announced over the gasps of the crowd.

"Peek!" Sunny cried.

"Nobody peek!" ordered the man with a beard but no hair. "Anyone who peeks will be turned over to the authorities!"

"Take off your blindfolds!" Violet begged the crowd. "Count Olaf is kidnapping Justice Strauss this very moment!"

"Hmm!" cried Justice Strauss in agreement, from behind the tape.

"Justice Strauss is enjoying a piece of salt-water taffy!" the woman with hair but no beard said quickly. "That's why she's talking in hmms!"

"She's not enjoying anything!" Klaus cried. "If there are any volunteers in the crowd, take off your blindfolds and help us!"

"The children are trying to trick you!" said the man with a beard but no hair. "Keep your blindfolds on!"

"Yes!" cried the woman with hair but no beard. "They're trying to get all noble people arrested by the authorities!"

"Real McCoy!" Sunny yelled.

"I think the children might be telling the truth," Jerome Squalor said hesitantly.

"Those brats are liars!" Esmé snapped. "They're worse than my ex-boyfriend!"

"I believe them!" Charles said, scratching at his blindfold. "They've experienced villainy before!"

"I don't!" Sir announced. The children could not tell if he was wearing a blindfold underneath the cloud of smoke that still hung over his head. "They're nothing but trouble!"

"They're telling the truth!" cried Frank, probably, unless it was Ernest.

"They're lying!" cried Ernest, most likely, although I suppose it could have been Frank.

"They're good students!" said Mr. Remora.

"They're lousy administrative assistants!" said Vice Principal Nero.

"They're bank robbers!" said Mrs. Bass, whose blindfold was covering her small, narrow mask.

"Bank robbers?" Mr. Poe asked. "Egad! Who said that?"

"They're guilty!" cried the man with a beard but no hair, although the High Court wasn't supposed to reach a verdict until all the evidence had been examined.

"They're innocent!" cried Hal.

"They're freaks!" screamed Hugo.

"They're twisted!" shrieked Colette.

"They're right-handed!" yelled Kevin.

"They're headlines!" screeched Geraldine Julienne.

"They're escaping!" said the woman with hair but no beard, and this, at least, was a true statement. Violet, Klaus, and Sunny realized that the crowd was going to do nothing that would stop Count Olaf from dragging Justice Strauss away from the trial, and that the people in the lobby would fail them, as so many noble people had failed them before. As the volunteers and villains argued around them, the children made their way quickly and stealthily away from the bench and toward Justice Strauss and Count Olaf, who was picking up the harpoon gun. If you've ever wanted one more cookie than people said you could have, then you know how difficult it is to move quickly and stealthily at the same time, but if you've had as much experience as the Baudelaires in dodging the activities of people who were shouting at you, then you know that with enough practice you can move quickly and stealthily just about anywhere, including across an enormous, domed lobby while a crowd calls for your capture.

"We must capture them!" called a voice in the crowd.

"It will take a village to capture the Baudelaires!" shrieked Mrs. Morrow. "We can't see them through our blindfolds!"

"We don't want to be guilty of contempt of court!" yelled Mr. Lesko. "Let's feel our way toward the hotel entrance so they can't escape!"

"The authorities are guarding the entrance!" the man with a beard but no hair reminded the crowd. "The Baudelaires are running toward the elevators! Capture them!"

"But don't capture anyone else who happens to be standing near the elevators!" added the woman with hair but no beard, looking hurriedly at Olaf. The sliding doors of an elevator began to open, and the Baudelaires moved as quickly and stealthily as they could through the crowd who were reaching out blindly in all directions.

"Search the entire hotel," said the villianous man, "and bring us anyone who you find suspicious!"

"We'll tell you if they're villains or not," said the villianous woman. "After all, you can't make such judgements yourselves!"

"*Wrong!*"

The enormous clock of the Hotel Denouement, the stuff of legend, announced one o'clock, thundering through the room of the blindfolded leading the blindfolded, just as the three siblings reached the elevators. Count Olaf had already dragged Justice Strauss inside and was hurriedly pressing the button that closes the elevator doors, but Sunny stuck out one of her feet and held them open, which is something only very brave people attempt. Olaf leaned forward to whisper threateningly at the Baudelaires.

"Let me go," he whispered threateningly, "or I'll announce to everyone where you are."

Olaf, however, was not the only person who could whisper threateningly. "Let us in," Violet whispered threateningly, "or we'll announce to everyone where *you* are."

"Hmm!" Justice Strauss said.

Count Olaf glared at the children, and the children glared back, until at last the villain stepped aside and let the Baudelaires join him and his prisoner in the elevator. "Going down?" he asked, and the children blinked. They had been so intent on escaping the crowd and reaching the judge that they hadn't considered exactly where they might go afterward.

"We're going wherever you go," Klaus said.

"I have a few errands to run," Olaf said. "Ha! First I'm going down to the basement, to retrieve the sugar bowl. Ha! Then I'm going up to the roof, to retrieve the Medusoid Mycelium. Ha! Then I'm going down to the lobby, to expose the fungus to everyone in the lobby. Ha! And then, finally, I'm going up to the roof, to escape without being seen by the authorities."

"You'll fail," Sunny said, and Olaf glared down at the youngest Baudelaire.

"Your mother told me the same thing," he said. "Ha! But one day, when I was seven years old—"

The elevator's doors slid open as it arrived at the basement, and the villain interrupted himself and quickly dragged Justice Strauss out into the hallway. "Follow me!" he called back to the Baudelaires. The children, of course, did not want to follow this horrid man any more than they wanted to put cream cheese in their hair, but they looked at one another and could not think of what else they could do.

"You can't retrieve the sugar bowl," Violet said. "You'll never open the Vernacularly Fastened Door."

"Can't I?" Olaf asked, stopping at Room 025. The lock was still stretched securely across the door, as it had been when Sunny left it. "This hotel is like an enormous library," the villain said, "but you can find any item in a library if you have one thing."

"Catalog?" Sunny asked.

"No," Count Olaf replied, and pointed the harpoon gun at the judge. "A hostage." With that, he turned to Justice Strauss and ripped the tape off her mouth very slowly, so it would sting as much as possible. "You're going to help me open this lock," he informed her, with a wicked smile.

"I will do nothing of the sort!" Justice Strauss replied. "The Baudelaires will help me drag you back up to the lobby, where justice can be served!"

"Justice isn't being served in the lobby," Olaf growled, "or anywhere else in the world!"

"Don't be so sure of that!" Justice Strauss said, and reached behind her back. The Baudelaires looked hopefully at what she was holding, but their hopes fell when they saw what it was. *"Odious Lusting After Finance,"* she read out loud, holding up Jerome Squalor's comprehensive history of injustice. "There's enough evidence in here to put you in jail for the rest of your life!"

"Justice Strauss," Violet said, "your fellow judges on the High Court are associates of Count Olaf. Those villains will never put Olaf in jail."

"It can't be!" Justice Strauss gasped. "I've known them for years! I've told them everything that was happening to you children, and they were always very interested!"

"Of course they were interested, you fool," Count Olaf said. "They passed along all that information to me, so I could catch up with the orphans! You've been helping me all along, without even knowing it! Ha!"

Justice Strauss leaned against an ornamental vase, and her eyes filled with tears. "I've failed you again, Baudelaires," she said. "No matter how I've tried to help you, I've only put you in more danger. I thought justice would be served if you told the High Court your story, but—"

"No one's interested in their story," Count Olaf said scornfully. "Even if you wrote down every last detail, no one would read such a dreadful thing. I've triumphed over the orphans and over any other person foolish or noble enough to stand in my way. It's the unraveling of my story, or, as the French say, the *noblesse oblige*."

"*Denouement*," Sunny corrected, but Olaf acted as though he had not heard, and turned his attention to the lock on the door.

"That idiot sub-sub said the first phrase is a description of a medical condition that all three Baudelaire children share," he muttered, and turned to Justice Strauss. "Tell me what it is, or prepare to eat harpoon."

"Never," Justice Strauss said. "I may have failed these children, but I won't fail V.F.D. You'll never get the sugar bowl, no matter what terrible threats you make."

"I'll tell you what the first phrase is," Klaus

said calmly, and his siblings looked at him in astonishment. Justice Strauss looked at him in amazement. Even Count Olaf seemed a little puzzled.

"You will?" he asked.

"Certainly," Klaus said. "It's just like you said, Count Olaf. Every noble person has failed us. Why should we protect the sugar bowl?"

"Klaus!" Violet and Sunny cried, in simultaneous astonishment.

"No!" Justice Strauss cried, in solitary amazement.

Count Olaf looked a little puzzled again, but then shrugged his dusty shoulders. "O.K.," he said, "tell me what medical condition you and your orphan siblings share."

"We're allergic to peppermints," Klaus said, and quickly typed A-L-L-E-R-G-I-C-T-O-P-E-P-P-E-R-M-I-N-T-S into the lock. Immediately, there was a muted clicking sound from the typewriter keyboard.

"It's warming up," Count Olaf said, in a

delighted wheeze. "Get out of the way, four-eyes! The second phrase is the weapon that left me an orphan, and I can type that one in myself. P-O-Y-Z—"

"Wait!" Klaus said, before Olaf could touch the keyboard. "That can't be right. Those letters don't spell anything."

"Spelling doesn't count," said the count.

"Yes, it does," Klaus said. "Tell me what the weapon is that left you an orphan, and I'll type it in for you."

Count Olaf gave Klaus a slow smile that made the Baudelaires shudder. "Certainly I'll tell you," he said. "It was poison darts."

Kláus looked at his sisters, and then in grim silence typed P-O-I-S-O-N-D-A-R-T-S into the lock, which began to buzz quietly. Count Olaf's eyes shone brightly as he stared at the wires of the lock, which began to shake as they stretched around the hinges of the laundry room door.

"It's working," he said, and ran his tongue

over his filthy teeth. "The sugar bowl is so close I can taste it!"

Klaus took his commonplace book from his pocket, and read his notes intently for a moment. Then he turned to Justice Strauss. "Give me that book, please," he said, pointing to Jerome Squalor's book. "The third phrase is the famous unfathomable question in the best-known novel by Richard Wright. Richard Wright was an American novelist of the realist school whose writings illuminated the disparities in race relations. It is likely his work is quoted in a comprehensive history of injustice."

"You can't read that entire book!" Count Olaf said. "The crowd will find us before you finish the first chapter!"

"I'll look in the index," Klaus said, "just like I did at Aunt Josephine's, when we decoded her note and found her hiding place."

"I always wondered how you did that," Olaf said, sounding almost as if he admired the middle

Baudelaire's research skills. Klaus paged to the back of the book, where the index can usually be found. An index, as I'm sure you know, is a list of everything a book contains, and where each item can be found.

"Wright, Richard," Klaus read aloud. "Unfathomable question in *Native Son*, page 581."

"That's the five hundred and eighty-first page," Count Olaf explained for no one's benefit, a phrase which here means "even though that was clear to everyone in the hallway."

Klaus flipped hurriedly to the proper page and scanned it quickly, his eyes blinking behind his glasses. "I found it," he said quietly. "It's quite an interesting question, actually."

"No one cares about interesting questions!" Olaf said. "Type it in this instant!"

Klaus smiled, and began typing furiously into the typewriter keyboard. His sisters stepped forward, and each of them put a hand on their brother's shoulder.

"Why do this?" Sunny asked.

"Sunny's right," Violet said. "Why are you helping Olaf get into the laundry room?"

The middle Baudelaire typed the last word into the keyboard, which was "T-O-P-P-L-I-N-G," and then looked at his sisters. "Because the sugar bowl isn't there," he said, and pushed open the door.

"What do you mean?" Count Olaf demanded. "Of course the sugar bowl is in there!"

"I'm afraid Olaf is right," Justice Strauss said. "You heard what Dewey said. When the crows were shot with the harpoon gun, they fell onto the birdpaper and dropped the sugar bowl into the funnel."

"So it would appear," Klaus said slyly.

"Enough nonsense!" Count Olaf shouted, waving his harpoon gun in the air and stomping into the laundry room. In just a few moments, however, it was clear that the middle Baudelaire had spoken the truth. The laundry room of the Hotel Denouement was very small, just large enough to hold a few washing and drying machines, some piles of dirty sheets, and a few plastic jugs of what were presumably some extremely flammable chemicals, just as Dewey had said. A metal tube hung over one corner of the ceiling, allowing steam from the machines to float up the tube and outside, but there was no sign that a sugar bowl had fallen through the funnel and dropped out the metal tube to the wooden floor of the laundry room. With a hoarse, angry roar, Count Olaf opened the doors of the washing and drying machines and slammed them closed, and then picked up the piles of dirty sheets and sent them tumbling onto the floor.

"Where is it?" he snarled, drops of spit flying from his furious mouth. "Where's the sugar bowl?"

"It's a secret," Klaus said. "A secret that died with Dewey Denouement."

Count Olaf turned to face the Baudelaire orphans, who had never seen him look this frightening. His eyes had never gleamed as brightly, and his smile had never been as peccant, a word which here means "so hungry for evil deeds as to be unhealthy." It was not unlike the face of Dewey had been as he sank into the water, as if the villain's own wickedness was causing him great pain. "He won't be the only volunteer who dies today," he said, in a terrible whisper. "I'll destroy every soul in his hotel, sugar bowl or no sugar bowl. I'll unleash the Medusoid Mycelium, and volunteers and villains alike will perish in agony. My comrades have failed me as often as my enemies, and I'm eager to be rid of them. Then I'll push that boat off the roof, and sail away with—"

"You can't push that boat off the roof," Violet said. "It would never survive the fall, due to the force of gravity."

"I suppose I'll have to add the force of gravity to my list of enemies," Olaf muttered.

"I'll get that boat off the roof," Violet said

calmly, and her siblings looked at her in astonishment. Justice Strauss looked at her in amazement. Even Count Olaf seemed a little puzzled.

"You will?" he asked.

"Certainly," Violet said. "It's just like you
said, Count Olaf. Every noble person has failed
us. Why shouldn't we help you escape?"

"Violet!" Klaus and Sunny cried, in simultaneous astonishment.

"No!" Justice Strauss cried, in solitary amazement.

Count Olaf still looked puzzled, but gave
the eldest Baudelaire a shrug. "O.K.," he said.
"What do you need?"

"A few of those dirty sheets," Violet said.
"I'll tie them together and make a drag chute,
just like I did in the Mortmain Mountains when
I stopped the caravan from falling off the mountain."

"I always wondered how you did that," Olaf
said, looking at the eldest Baudelaire as if he
respected her inventing skills. Violet walked

into the laundry room and gathered some sheets into her arms, trying to choose the least dirty of the bunch.

"Let's go to the roof," she said quietly. Her siblings stepped forward, and each of them put a hand on their sister's shoulder.

"Why do this?" Sunny asked.

"Sunny's right," Klaus said. "Why are you helping Olaf escape?"

The eldest Baudelaire looked at the sheets in her hand, and then at her siblings. "Because he'll take us with him," she said.

"Why would I do that?" Olaf asked.

"Because you need more than a one-person crew," Violet said slyly, "and we need to leave this hotel without being spotted by the authorities."

"I suppose that's true," Olaf said. "Well, you would have ended up in my clutches in any case. Come along."

"Not yet," Sunny said. "One more thing."

Everyone stared at the youngest Baudelaire,

who was wearing an expression so unfathomable that even her siblings could not tell what she was thinking. "One more thing?" Count Olaf repeated, staring down at Sunny. "What could that be?"

The two eldest Baudelaires looked at their sister, and felt a cold ripple in their stomachs, as if a stone had somehow been dropped straight into the siblings. It is very difficult to make one's way in this world without being wicked at one time or another, when the world's way is so wicked to begin with. When unfathomable situations arose in the lives of the Baudelaires, and they did not know what to do, the children often felt as if they were balancing very delicately on top of something very fragile and very dangerous, and that if they weren't careful they might fall a very long way into a sea of wickedness. Violet felt this delicate balance when she offered to help Count Olaf escape, even though it meant that she and her siblings could escape, too, and Klaus felt this delicate balance when he helped Olaf unlock the laundry room door, even though the sugar bowl was not to be found inside. And of course, all three Baudelaire orphans felt this delicate balance when they thought about Dewey Denouement, and that terrible instant when the weapon in their hands brought about his death. But as Sunny answered Count Olaf's question, the clock of the Hotel Denouement struck two *Wrong!*s, and her siblings wondered if they had lost their balance at last and were tumbling away from all the noble people in the world.

"Burn down hotel," Sunny said, and all three Baudelaire orphans felt as if they were falling.

CHAPTER
Thirteen

"Ha!" Count Olaf crowed. "This takes the cake!" He was using an expression which here means "I find this especially amusing and outrageous!" although Dewey Denouement's underwater catalog contains a list of twenty-seven cakes that

alog contains a list of twenty-seven cakes that although Dewey Denouement's underwater catalog contains this especially amusing and outrageous!" He was using an expression which here means "I *"Ha!"* Count Olaf crowed. "This takes the cake!"

Thirteen
CHAPTER

Olaf has stolen. With a look of treacherous glee he reached down and patted Sunny Baudelaire on the head, using the hand that wasn't clutching the harpoon gun. "After all this time, the littlest orphan wants to follow in my footsteps!" he cried. "I knew I was a good guardian after all!"

"You're not a good guardian," Violet said, "and Sunny's not an arsonist. My sister doesn't know what she's saying."

"Burn down hotel," Sunny insisted.

"Are you feeling all right, Sunny?" Klaus asked, peering into his sister's eyes. He was worried that the Medusoid Mycelium, which had threatened the life of the youngest Baudelaire just days ago, was affecting her in some sinister way. Klaus had researched a way to dilute the treacherous fungus, but he wondered now if dilution was not enough.

"I feel fine," Sunny said. "Burn down hotel."

"That's my girl!" Count Olaf cried. "I only

wish Carmelita had your spunk! With all the errands I had to do, burning down this hotel hadn't even occurred to me. But even when you're very busy, you should always take time for your hobbies."

"Your hobbies," Justice Strauss said, "are nothing but villainy, Count Olaf. The Baudelaires may want to join you in wickedness, but I'll do anything in my power to stop you."

"There's nothing in your power," Olaf sneered. "Your fellow judges are comrades of mine, your fellow volunteers are running around the lobby of this hotel wearing blindfolds, and I have the harpoon gun."

"I have a comprehensive history of injustice!" Justice Strauss cried. "This book should be good for something!"

The villain did not continue his argument, but merely pointed the weapon at the judge. "You orphans will start the fire here in the laundry room," he said, "while I make sure Justice Strauss doesn't stop us."

"Yes, sir," Sunny said, and reached for her siblings' hands.

"No!" Justice Strauss cried.

"Why are you doing this, Sunny?" Violet asked her sister. "You're going to hurt innocent people!"

"Why are you helping Count Olaf burn down this building?" Klaus cried.

Sunny looked at the laundry room, and then up at her siblings. In silence, she shook her head, as if this were not the time to discuss such matters. "Help me," she said, and she did not have to say anything more. Although Violet and Klaus found their sister's actions unfathomable, they followed her into the laundry room as Olaf uttered a succinct laugh of triumph.

"Ha!" Count Olaf cried. "Pay attention, orphans, and I'll teach you some of my best tricks. First, spread those dirty sheets all over the floor. Then, take those jugs of extremely flammable chemicals and pour them all over the sheets."

In silence, Violet spread the rest of the sheets over the laundry room's wooden floor, while Klaus and Sunny walked over to the plastic jugs, opened them, and spilled them all over the sheets. A strong, bitter smell wafted from the laundry room as the children turned to Olaf and asked what was next.

"What is next?" Sunny asked.

"Next is a match and some kindling," Olaf replied, and reached into his pocket with the hand that wasn't holding the gun. "I always carry matches on my person," he said, "just as my enemies always carry kindling." He leaned forward and snatched *Odious Lusting After Finance* out of Justice Strauss's hands. "This book *is* good for something," he said, and tossed it into the center of the dirty sheets, narrowly missing the siblings as they walked into the hallway. Jerome Squalor's book opened as it landed, and the children saw what looked like a carefully drawn diagram, with arrows and dotted lines and a paragraph of notation underneath.

The Baudelaires leaned forward to see if they could read what the injustice expert had written, and caught only the word "passageway" before Olaf lit a match and tossed it expertly onto the page. The paper caught on fire at once, and the book began to burn.

"Oh," Sunny said quietly, and leaned against her siblings. All three Baudelaires, and the adults standing with them, stared into the laundry room in silence.

The burning of a book is a sad, sad sight, for even though a book is nothing but ink and paper, it feels as if the ideas contained in the book are disappearing as the pages turn to ashes and the cover and binding—which is the term for the stitching and glue that holds the pages together—blacken and curl as the flames do their wicked work. When someone is burning a book, they are showing utter contempt for all of the thinking that produced its ideas, all of the labor that went into its words and sentences, and all of the trouble that befell the author, from the swarm of termites that tried to destroy his notes, to the large boulder that someone rolled onto the illustrator as he sat by the edge of the pond waiting for the delivery of the manuscript. Justice Strauss gazed at the book with a shocked frown, perhaps thinking of Jerome Squalor's research and all the villains it might have brought to justice. Count Olaf stared at the book with a smug smile, perhaps thinking of all of the other libraries he had destroyed. But you and I know there is no "perhaps" about what the Baudelaire orphans were thinking as they stared at the flames devouring the comprehensive history of injustice. Violet, Klaus, and Sunny were thinking of the fire that took their parents and their home and dropped them into the world to fend for themselves, a phrase which here means "go first from guardian to guardian, and then from desperate situation to desperate situation, trying to survive and solve the mysteries that hung over their heads like smoke." The Baudelaire orphans were thinking of the first fire that had come into their lives, and wondering if this one would be the last.

"We'd best get away from here," Count Olaf said, breaking the silence. "In my experience, once the flames reach the chemicals, the fire will spread very quickly. I'm afraid the cocktail party will be canceled, but if we hurry, there's still time to infect the guests of this hotel with the Medusoid Mycelium before we escape. Ha! To the elevators!"

Twirling the harpoon gun in his hands, the villain strode down the hallway, dragging the judge as he went, and the Baudelaires hurried to follow. When they reached the elevator, the children looked at a sign posted near one of the ornamental vases. The sign was identical to one posted in the lobby, and it is a sign you have probably seen yourself. IN CASE OF FIRE, it said, in fancy script, USE STAIRS. DO NOT USE ELEVATOR.

"Stairs," Sunny said, pointing at the sign.

"Ignore that," Olaf said scornfully, punching

the button to summon an elevator.

"Dangerous," Sunny pointed out. "Take the stairs."

"You may have had the idea to burn down the hotel," Count Olaf said, "but I'm still the boss, baby! We won't get to the fungus in time if we take the stairs! We're taking the elevator!"

"Drat," Sunny said quietly, and frowned in thought. Violet and Klaus looked at their sister curiously, wondering why a child who didn't mind setting a hotel on fire would be upset over something like an elevator. But then Sunny gazed up at her siblings with a sly smile, and uttered one word that made everything clear.

"Preludio," she said, and after a moment her siblings grinned.

"*What?*" Olaf asked sharply, and punched the button over and over again, which never helps.

"What my sister means," Violet said, "is that she appreciates the lesson on setting fires," but that is not what the youngest Baudelaire meant at all. By "Preludio," her siblings knew, Sunny was referring to the Hotel Preludio, and the weekend vacation the entire Baudelaire family had spent there. As Kit Snicket had mentioned, the Hotel Preludio was a lovely place, and I am happy to report that it is still standing, like a small mercy, and that its ballroom still has its famous chandeliers, which are shaped like enormous jellyfish and move up and down in time to the music that the orchestra plays, and that the bookstore in the lobby still specializes in the work of American novelists of the realist school, and the outdoor swimming pool is still as beautiful as it ever was, its reflection of the hotel windows shimmering whenever anyone dives in to swim laps. But the Baudelaire orphans were not remembering the chandeliers, or the bookstore, or even the swimming pool, where Sunny first learned to blow bubbles. They were remembering a prank their father had taught them, when he was in one of his whimsical moods, that can be played in any elevator. The prank, a word which here means "joke played on someone with whom you are sharing an elevator," is best played at the moment when you are about to get off the elevator, and your fellow passengers are heading to a higher story. The Baudelaires' mother had objected to their father teaching them such a prank, as she said it was undignified, but their father had pointed out it was no more undignified than doing magic tricks with dinner rolls, which their mother had done that very morning in the hotel restaurant, and she reluctantly agreed to participate in the prank. This particular moment in the Baudelaires' lives, of course, was not the best one for a prank, but Violet and Klaus saw immediately what their sister had in mind, and when the sliding doors opened and Count Olaf stomped inside the elevator, the three Baudelaires followed him and immediately pressed every single button. When the Baudelaires' father had done this after exiting the elevator, it meant that the remaining passenger, a tiresome woman named Eleanora, had been forced to visit every story on the way up to her room, but here in the Hotel Denouement, the prank served a dual purpose, a phrase which here means "enabled the Baudelaires to do two things at once."

"What are you doing?" Olaf shrieked. "I'll never reach the Medusoid Mycelium in time to poison everyone!"

"We'll be able to warn as many people as possible that the building is on fire!" cried Justice Strauss.

"Dual purpose," Sunny said, and shared a small smile with her siblings as the elevator reached the lobby and opened its doors. The enormous, domed room was nearly empty, and the Baudelaires could see that everyone had followed the advice of the two wicked judges of the High Court, and were wandering blindfolded around the hotel.

"Fire!" cried Violet immediately, knowing the doors would slide shut in an instant. "Attention everyone! There's a fire in the hotel! Please leave at once!"

The man with a beard but no hair was standing nearby, with his hand on Jerome Squalor's shoulder so he could push the injustice expert around. "Fire?" he said, in his strange, hoarse voice. "Good work, Olaf!"

"What do you mean, good work?" demanded Jerome, a frown appearing below his blindfold.

"I meant to say, 'there's Olaf!'" the man said hurriedly, pushing Jerome in the direction of the elevator. "Capture him! He needs to be brought to the authorities!"

"Olaf is here?" asked probably Frank, who was feeling his way along the wall along with his brother. "I'm going to capture him!"

"Where are the Baudelaires?" demanded probably Ernest. "I'm going to capture them!"

"In the elevator!" shouted the woman with hair but no beard from across the lobby, but the sliding doors were already closing.

"Call the fire department!" Violet cried desperately.

"Which one?" was the reply, but the children could not tell if it came from Frank or Ernest, and the doors slid shut on this one last glimpse of the villains and volunteers before the elevator began its rise to the second story.

"Those judges promised that if I waited until tomorrow I'd see all my enemies destroyed," Count Olaf grumbled, "and now they're trying to capture me. I knew they'd fail me some day."

The Baudelaires did not have time to point out that Olaf had also failed the judges, by planning to poison them, along with everyone else in the lobby, with the Medusoid Mycelium, because the elevator immediately stopped on the second story and opened its doors.

"There's a fire in the hotel!" Klaus called into the hallway. "Everyone leave at once!"

"A fire?" said Esmé Squalor. The Baudelaires were surprised to see that this treacherous woman was still wearing her blindfold, but perhaps she had decided that pieces of black cloth were in. "Who said that?"

"It's Klaus Baudelaire," Klaus Baudelaire said. "You need to get out of the hotel!"

"Don't listen to that cakesniffer!" cried Carmelita Spats, who was running a hand over an ornamental vase. "He's just trying to escape from us! Let's take off our blindfolds and peek!"

"Don't take off your blindfolds!" cried Count Olaf. "Those Baudelaires are guilty of contempt of court, and they're trying to trick you into joining them! There's no fire! Whatever you do, don't leave the hotel!"

"We're not tricking you!" Klaus said. "Olaf is tricking you! Please believe us!"

"I don't know who to believe," Esmé said scornfully. "You orphans are as dishonest as my ex-boyfriend."

"Leave us alone!" Carmelita ordered, bumping into a wall. "We can find our own way!"

The doors slid shut before the Baudelaires

could argue any further, and indeed the children never argued with either unpleasant female again. In a moment, the elevator arrived at the third story, and Sunny raised her voice so that she could be heard by anyone, treacherous or noble, in the hallway.

"Fire!" she cried. "Use stairs. Do not use elevator!"

"Sunny Baudelaire?" Mr. Poe called, recognizing the child's voice. The banker was facing the entirely wrong direction, and holding a white handkerchief up to his black blindfold. "Don't add the false reporting of fire to your list of crimes! You're already guilty of contempt of court, and perhaps murder!"

"It's not false!" Justice Strauss exclaimed. "There really is a fire, Mr. Poe! Leave this hotel!"

"I can't leave," Mr. Poe replied, coughing into his handkerchief. "I'm still in charge of the Baudelaires' affairs, and their parents' fort—"

The elevator doors closed before Mr. Poe

could finish his word, and the Baudelaires were taken away from the banker one last time, and with each stop of the elevator, I'm sorry to say, it was more or less the same. The Baudelaires saw Mrs. Bass on the third story, still wearing her small blond wig like a snowcap on the top of a mountain peak, and her blindfold, stretched over her small, narrow mask, and they saw Mr. Remora, who was wandering around the seventh story with Vice Principal Nero. They saw Geraldine Julienne, who was using her microphone the way some blind people use a cane, and they saw Charles and Sir, who were holding hands so as not to lose one another, and they saw Hugo and Colette and Kevin, who were holding the birdpaper Klaus had hung outside the window of the sauna, and they saw Mr. Lesko arguing with Mrs. Morrow, and they saw a man with a guitar making friends with a woman in a crow-shaped hat, and they saw many people they did not recognize, either as volunteers or as villains, who were wandering the hallways of the hotel to capture anyone they might find suspicious. Some of these people believed the Baudelaires when they told them the news of the fire, and some of these people believed Count Olaf when he told them that the Baudelaires were lying, and some of these people believed Justice Strauss when she told them that Count Olaf was lying when he said the Baudelaires were lying when they told them the news of the fire. But the elevator's stop on each story of the hotel was very brief, and the children had only a glimpse of each of these people. They heard Mrs. Bass mutter something about a getaway car, and they heard Mr. Remora wonder something about fried bananas. They heard Nero worry about his violin case, and Geraldine squeal about headlines, and they heard Charles and Sir bicker over whether or not fires were good for the lumber industry. They heard Hugo ask if the plan for the hors d'ouvres was still in operation, and they heard Colette ask about plucking the feathers off crows, and they heard Kevin complain that

he didn't know whether to hold the birdpaper
in his right hand or his left hand, and they heard
Mr. Lesko insult Mrs. Morrow, and the bearded
man sing a song to the woman with the crow-
shaped hat, and they heard a man call for Bruce
and a woman call for her mother and dozens of
people whisper to and shout at, argue with and
agree upon, angrily accuse and meekly defend,
furiously compliment and kindly insult dozens
of other people, both inside and outside the
Hotel Denouement, whose names the Baudelaires recognized, forgot, and had never heard
before. Each story had its story, and each story's
story was unfathomable in the Baudelaire
orphans' short journey, and many of the stories'
stories are unfathomable to me, even after all
these lonely years and all this lonely research.
Perhaps some of these stories are clearer to you,
because you have spied upon the people
involved. Perhaps Mrs. Bass has changed her
name and lives near you, or perhaps Mr.
Remora's name is the same, and he lives far

away. Perhaps Nero now works as a grocery store clerk, or Geraldine Julienne now teaches arts and crafts. Perhaps Charles and Sir are no longer partners, and you have had the occasion to study one of them as he sat across from you on a bus, or perhaps Hugo, Colette, and Kevin are still comrades, and you have followed these unfathomable people after noticing that one of them used both hands equally. Perhaps Mr. Lesko is now your neighbor, or Mrs. Morrow is now your sister, or your mother, or your aunt or wife or even your husband. Perhaps the noise you hear outside your door is a bearded man trying to climb into your window, or perhaps it is a woman in a crow-shaped hat hailing a taxi. Perhaps you have spotted the managers of the Hotel Denouement, or the judges of the High Court, or the waiters of Café Salmonella or the Anxious Clown, or perhaps you have met an expert on injustice or become one yourself. Perhaps the people in your unfathomable life, and their unfathomable stories, are clear to you as

you make your way in the world, but when the
elevator stopped for the last time, and the doors
slid open to reveal the tilted roof of the Hotel
Denouement, the Baudelaires felt as if they
were balancing very delicately on a mysterious
and perplexing heap of unfathomable mysteries. They did not know who would survive the
fire they had helped set, and who would perish.
They did not know who thought they were volunteers and who thought they were villains, or
who believed they were innocent and who
believed they were guilty. And they did not
know if their own observations, errands, and
deeds meant that they were noble, or wicked,
or somewhere in between. As they stepped out
of the elevator and walked across the rooftop
sunbathing salon, the Baudelaire orphans felt as
if their entire lives were like a book, filled with
crucial information, that had been set aflame,
like the comprehensive history of injustice that
was now just ashes in a fire growing more enormous by the second.

"Look!" cried Count Olaf, leaning over the edge of the hotel and pointing down. The Baudelaires looked, expecting to see the enormous, calm surface of the pond reflecting the Hotel Denouement back at them like an enormous mirror. But the air was stained with patches of thick, black smoke that poured out of the basement windows as the fire began to spread, and the surface of the pond looked like a series of tiny mirrors, each broken into strange, unfathomable shapes. Here and there, among the smoke and mirrors, the children could see the tiny figures running this way and that, but could not tell if they were the authorities on the ground, or people in the hotel running to escape from the blaze.

Olaf continued to gaze downward, and the Baudelaires could not tell if he looked pleased or disappointed. "Thanks to you orphans," he said, "it's too late to destroy everyone with the Medusoid Mycelium, but at least we got to start a fire."

Justice Strauss was still gazing at the smoke pouring from the windows and rising into the sky, and her expression was equally unfathomable. "Thanks to you orphans," she said quietly to the Baudelaires, "this hotel will be destroyed by fire, but at least we stopped Olaf from releasing the fungus."

"The fire isn't burning very quickly," Olaf said. "Many people will escape."

"The fire isn't burning slowly, either," Justice Strauss said. "Some people won't."

The Baudelaire orphans looked at one another, but before anyone could say anything further, the entire building trembled, and the children had to struggle to keep their balance on the tilted roof. The shiny sunbathing mats tumbled across the salon, and the water in the swimming pool splashed against the side of the large, wooden boat, dampening the figurehead of the octopus attacking a man in a diving suit.

"The fire is weakening the structural foundations of the building," Violet said.

"We have to get out of here," Klaus said.

"Pronto," Sunny said.

Without another word the Baudelaires turned from the adults and strode quickly toward the boat. Shifting the pile of sheets into one hand, Violet took off her concierge hat, reached into her pocket, and found the ribbon Kit Snicket had given her, which she used to tie up her hair. Klaus reached into his pocket and found his commonplace book, which he began to flip through. Sunny did not reach into her pocket, but she scraped her sharp teeth together thoughtfully, as she suspected they might be needed.

Violet stared critically at the boat. "I'll attach the drag chute to the figurehead," she said. "I should be able to tie a Devil's Tongue knot around the helmet of the diver." She paused for a moment. "That's where the Medusoid Mycelium is hidden," she said. "Count Olaf kept it there, where no one would think of looking."

Klaus stared critically at his notes. "I'll angle the sail to catch the wind," he said. "Otherwise, a heavy object like this would fall straight down into the water." He paused for a moment, too. "That's what happened to the sugar bowl," he said. "Dewey Denouement let everyone think it had fallen into the laundry room, so no one would find it in the pond."

"Spatulas as oars," Sunny said, pointing to the implements that Hugo had used to flip over the sunbathers.

"Good idea," Violet agreed and gazed out to the gray, troubled waters of the sea. "Maybe our friends will find us. Hector should be flying this way, with Kit Snicket and the Quagmires."

"And Fiona," Klaus added.

"No," Sunny said.

"What do you mean?" Violet asked, stepping carefully from the edge of the pool onto the side of the boat, where she began to climb a rope ladder up to the figurehead.

"They said they would arrive by Thursday,"

Klaus said, helping Sunny climb aboard and then stepping onto the boat himself. The deck was about the size of a large mattress, big enough to hold the Baudelaires and perhaps one or two more passengers. "It's Wednesday afternoon."

"The fire," Sunny said, and pointed at the smoke as it rose toward the sky.

The two older Baudelaires gasped. They had almost forgotten that Kit had told them she would be watching the skies, looking for a signal that would cancel Thursday's gathering.

"That's why you thought of lighting the fire," Violet said, hurriedly tying the sheets around the figurehead. "It's a signal."

"V.F.D. will see it," Klaus said, "and know that all their hopes have gone up in smoke."

Sunny nodded. "The last safe place," she said, "is safe no more."

It was an impressive sentence for the youngest Baudelaire, but a sad one.

"Maybe our friends will find us anyway,"

Violet said. "They might be the last noble people we know."

"If they're truly noble," Klaus said, "they might not want to be our friends."

Violet nodded, and her eyes filled with tears. "You're right," she admitted. "We killed a man."

"Accident," Sunny said firmly.

"And burned down a hotel," Klaus said.

"Signal," Sunny said.

"We had good reasons," Violet said, "but we still did bad things."

"We want to be noble," Klaus said, "but we've had to be treacherous."

"Noble enough," Sunny said, but the building trembled again, as if shaking its head in disagreement. Violet hung on to the figurehead and Klaus and Sunny hung on to each other as the boat bumped against the sides of the swimming pool.

"Help us!" Violet cried to the adults, who were still staring at the rising smoke. "Grab those spatulas, and push the boat to the edge of the roof!"

"Don't boss me around!" Olaf growled, but he followed the judge to a corner of the roof where the spatulas lay, their mirrors reflecting the afternoon sun and the sky as it darkened with smoke. Each adult grabbed one spatula, and poked at the boat the way you might poke at a spider you were trying to get out of your bathtub. *Bump! Bump!* The sailboat bumped against the edge of the pool, and then jostled its way out of the pool, where it slowly slid, with a loud scraping sound, to the far edge of the roof. The Baudelaires hung on tightly as the front half of the boat kept sliding across the mirrors of the salon, until it was hanging over nothing but the smoky air. The boat tipped this way and that, in a delicate balance between the roof of the hotel and the sea below.

"Climb aboard!" Violet cried, giving her knots one last tug.

"Of course I'll climb aboard!" Olaf announced, narrowing his eyes at the helmet of the figurehead. "I'm the captain of this boat!" He threw his spatula onto the deck, narrowly missing Klaus and Sunny, and then bounded onto the ship, making it teeter wildly on the edge of the building.

"You too, Justice Strauss!' Klaus called, but the judge just put down her spatula and looked sadly at the children.

"No," she said, and the children could see she was crying. "I won't go. It's not right."

"What else can we do?" Sunny said, but Justice Strauss just shook her head.

"I won't run from the scene of a crime," she said. "You children should come with me, and we'll explain everything to the authorities."

"They might not believe us," Violet said, readying the drag chute, "or there might be enemies lurking in their ranks, like the villains in the High Court."

"Perhaps," the judge said, "but that's no excuse for running away."

Count Olaf gave his former neighbor a scornful look, and then turned to the Baudelaires. "Let her burn to a crisp if she wants," he said, "but it's time for us to go."

Justice Strauss took a deep breath, and then stepped forward and put her hand on the hideous wooden carving, as if she meant to drag the whole boat back onto the hotel. "There are people who say that criminal behavior is the destiny of children from a broken home," she said, through her tears. "Don't make this your destiny, Baudelaires."

Klaus stood at the mast, adjusting the controls of the sail. "This boat," he said, "is the only home we have."

"I've been following you all this time," she said, her grip tightening on the figurehead. "You've always been just out of my grasp, from the moment Mr. Poe took you away from the theater in his car to the moment Kit Snicket took you through the hedges in her taxi. I won't let you go, Baudelaires!"

Sunny stepped toward the judge, and for one moment her siblings thought she was going to step off the boat. But then she merely looked into the judge's weeping eyes, and gave her a very sad smile.

"Good-bye," she said, and the Baudelaire opened her mouth and bit the hand of justice. With a cry of pain and frustration, Justice Strauss let go of the figurehead, and the building trembled again, sending the judge tumbling to the ground, and the boat tumbling off the roof, just as the clock of the Hotel Denouement announced the hour for the very last time.

Wrong! Wrong! Wrong! The clock struck three times, and the three Baudelaires screamed as they hurtled toward the sea, and even Count Olaf cried "Mommy!" as it seemed for a terrible moment that their luck had run out at last, and that the boat would not survive the fall, due to the force of gravity. But then Violet let go of the dirty sheets, and the drag chute billowed into the air, looking almost like another patch of smoke against the sky, and Klaus moved the sail to catch the wind, and the boat stopped falling and started to glide, the way a bird will catch the wind, and rest its wings for a few moments, particularly if it is tired from carrying something heavy and important. For a moment, the boat floated down through the air, like something in a magical story, and even in their panic and fear the Baudelaires could not help marveling at the way they were escaping. Finally, with a mighty *splash!* the boat landed in the ocean, quite a distance from the burning hotel. For another terrible moment, it felt like the boat was going to sink into the water, just as Dewey Denouement had sunk into the pond, guarding his underwater catalog and all its secrets, and leaving the woman he loved pregnant and distraught. But the sail caught the wind, and the figurehead righted itself, and Olaf picked up his spatula and handed it to Sunny.

"Start rowing," he ordered, and then began

to cackle, his eyes shining bright. "You're in my clutches at last, orphans," he said. "We're all in the same boat."

The Baudelaires looked at the villain, and then at the shore. For a moment they were tempted to jump overboard and swim back toward the city and away from Olaf. But when they looked at the smoke, pouring from the windows of the hotel, and the flames, curling around the lilies and moss that someone had grown with such care on the walls, they knew it would be just as dangerous on land. They could see the tiny figures of people standing outside the hotel, fiercely pointing toward the sea, and they saw the building tremble. It seemed that the Hotel Denouement would soon be sent toppling, and the children wanted to be far away. Dewey had promised them that they wouldn't be at sea anymore, but at this moment the sea, for the Baudelaires, was the last safe place.

Richard Wright, an American novelist of the realist school, asks a famous unfathomable question in his best-known novel, *Native Son*. "Who knows when some slight shock," he asks, "disturbing the delicate balance between social order and thirsty aspiration, shall send the skyscrapers in our cities toppling?" It is a difficult question to read, almost as if it is in some sort of code, but after much research I have been able to make some sense of its mysterious words. "Social order," for instance, is a phrase which may refer to the systems people use to organize their lives, such as the Dewey Decimal System, or the blindfolded procedures of the High Court. And "thirsty aspiration" is a phrase which may refer to things people want, such as the Baudelaire fortune, or the sugar bowl, or a safe place that lonely and exhausted orphans can call home. So when Mr. Wright asks his question, he might be wondering if a small event, such as a stone dropping into a pond, can cause ripples in the systems of the world, and tremble the things that people want, until all this rippling and trembling brings down something enormous, such as a building.

The Baudelaires, of course, did not have a copy of *Native Son* on the wooden boat that served as their new home, but as they gazed across the water at the Hotel Denouement, they were asking themselves a question not unlike Mr. Wright's. Violet, Klaus, and Sunny wondered about all the things, large and small, that they had done. They wondered about their observations as flaneurs, which left so many mysteries unsolved. They wondered about all their errands as concierges, which brought about so much trouble. And they wondered if they were still the noble volunteers they wanted to be, or if, as the fire made its wicked way through the hotel, and the building threatened to topple, it was their destiny to become something else. The Baudelaire orphans stood in the same boat as Count Olaf, the notorious villain, and looked out at the sea, where they hoped they could find their noble friends, and wondered what else they could do, and who they might become.

© Meredith Heuer

LEMONY SNICKET has been chronicling the lives of the Baudelaire children with only occasional breaks for food, rest, and court-appointed swordfights. His hobbies include nervous apprehension, increasing dread, and wondering if his enemies were right after all.

Visit him on the web at www.lemonysnicket.com.

BRETT HELQUIST was born in Ganado, Arizona, grew up in Orem, Utah, and now lives in Brooklyn, New York. He earned a bachelor's degree in fine arts from Brigham Young University and has been illustrating ever since. Sometimes, he finds his work so distressing that he sends himself flowers, but it never helps.

To My Kind Editor,

The end is near.

With all due respect,

Lemony Snicket